WIN'S
RIES
OF THE CELTS

DRAWING
Eduardo Ocaña

SCRIPT
Sylvain Runberg

COLOUR WORK
Tariq Bellaoui

CINEBOOK
The 9th Art Publisher

Original title: Les carnets de Darwin 1 – L'œil des celtes

Original edition: © Editions du Lombard (Dargaud-Lombard SA) 2010
by Sylvain Runberg & Eduardo Ocaña
www.lelombard.com

English translation: © 2011 Cinebook Ltd

Translator: Jerome Saincantin
Lettering and text layout: Imadjinn
Printed in Spain by Just Colour Graphic

This edition first published in Great Britain in 2011 by
Cinebook Ltd
56 Beech Avenue
Canterbury, Kent
CT4 7TA
www.cinebook.com

A CIP catalogue record for this book
is available from the British Library

ISBN 978-1-84918-095-5

9th CINEBOOK
The 9th Art Publisher

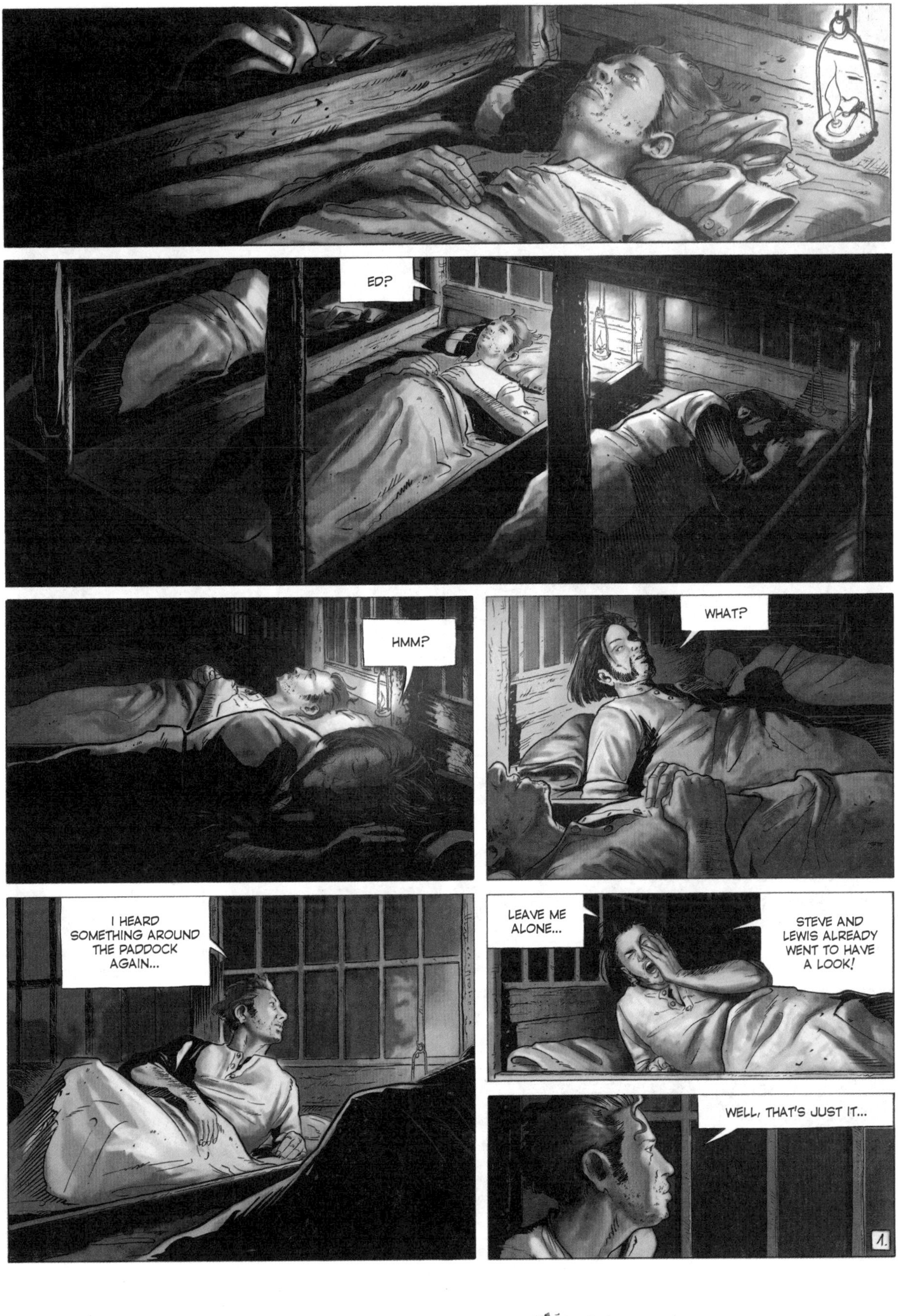
ED?
HMM?
WHAT?
I HEARD SOMETHING AROUND THE PADDOCK AGAIN...
LEAVE ME ALONE...
STEVE AND LEWIS ALREADY WENT TO HAVE A LOOK!
WELL, THAT'S JUST IT...
1.

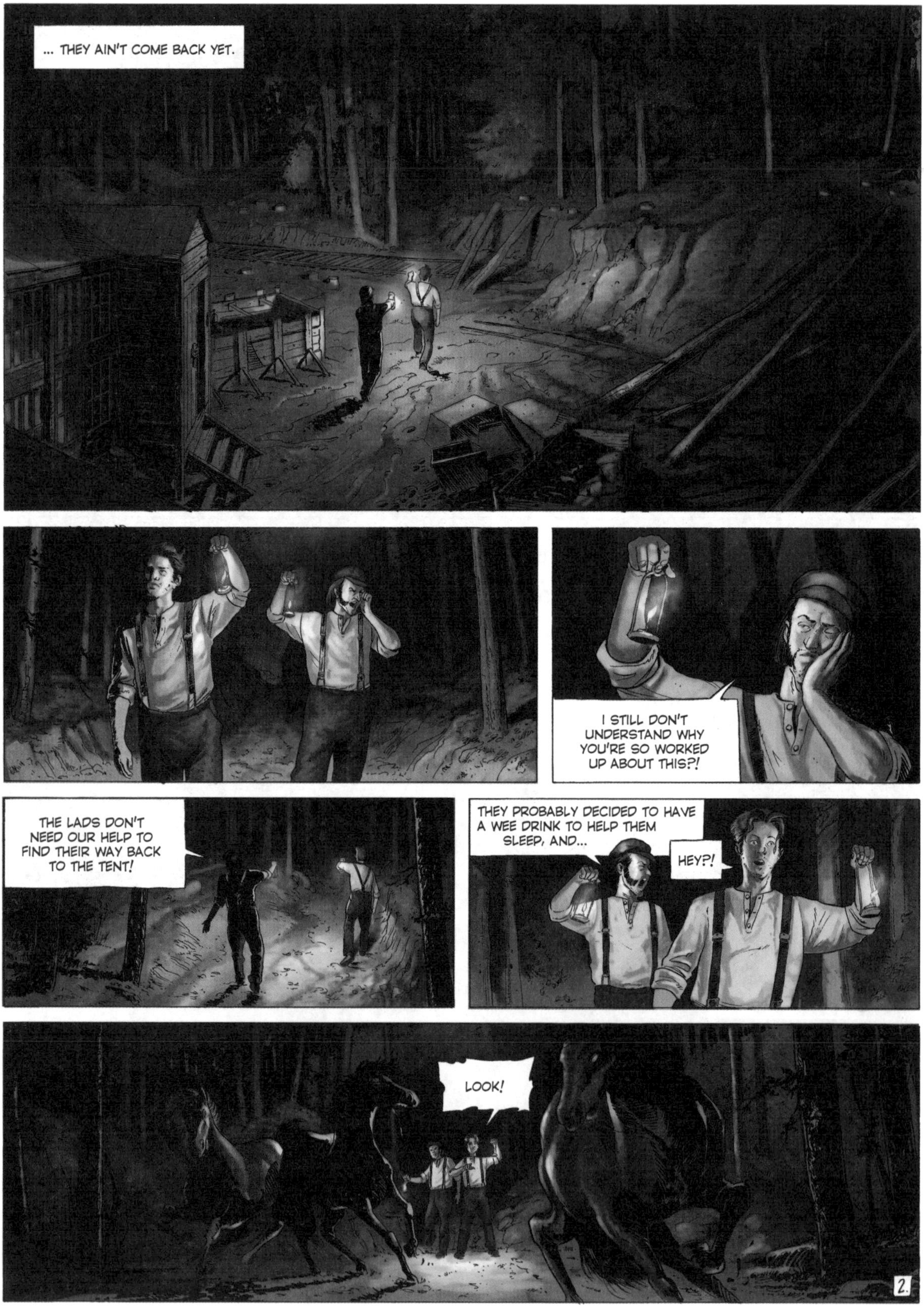
... THEY AIN'T COME BACK YET.
I STILL DON'T UNDERSTAND WHY YOU'RE SO WORKED UP ABOUT THIS?!
THE LADS DON'T NEED OUR HELP TO FIND THEIR WAY BACK TO THE TENT!
THEY PROBABLY DECIDED TO HAVE A WEE DRINK TO HELP THEM SLEEP, AND...
HEY?!
LOOK!
2.

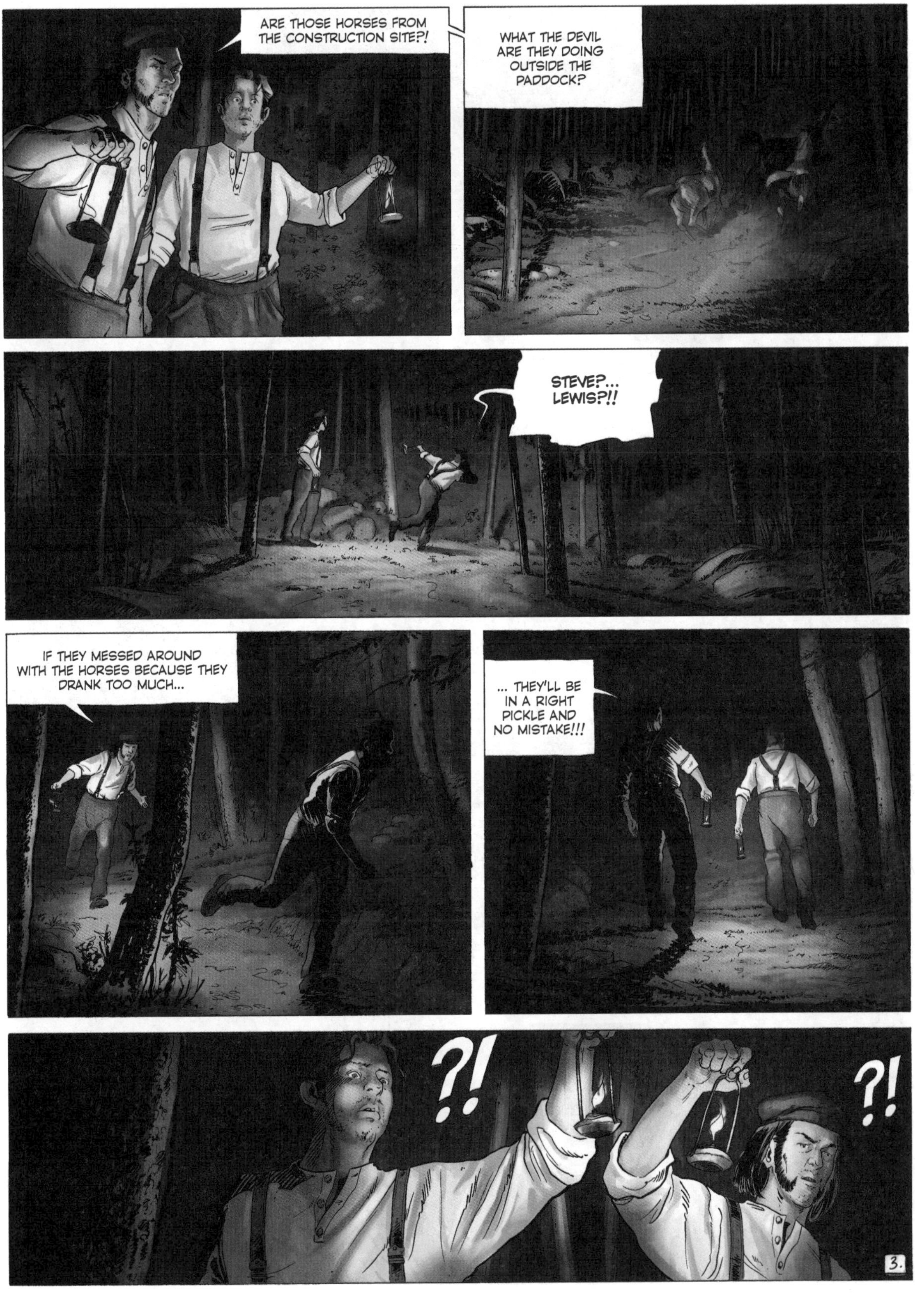
ARE THOSE HORSES FROM THE CONSTRUCTION SITE?!
WHAT THE DEVIL ARE THEY DOING OUTSIDE THE PADDOCK?
STEVE?... LEWIS?!!
IF THEY MESSED AROUND WITH THE HORSES BECAUSE THEY DRANK TOO MUCH...
... THEY'LL BE IN A RIGHT PICKLE AND NO MISTAKE!!!
?!
?!
3.

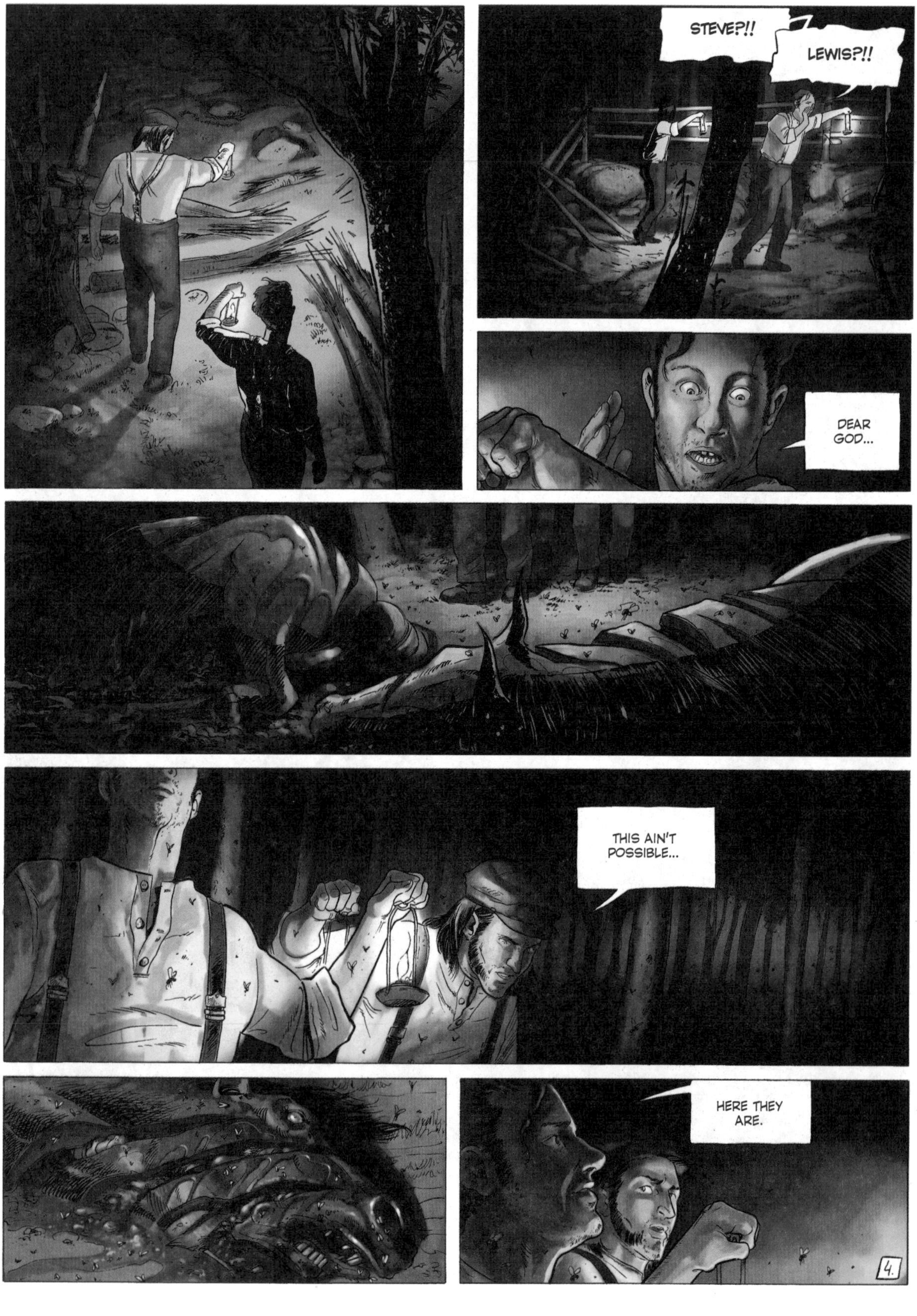
STEVE?!!
LEWIS?!!
DEAR GOD...
THIS AIN'T POSSIBLE...
HERE THEY ARE.
4.

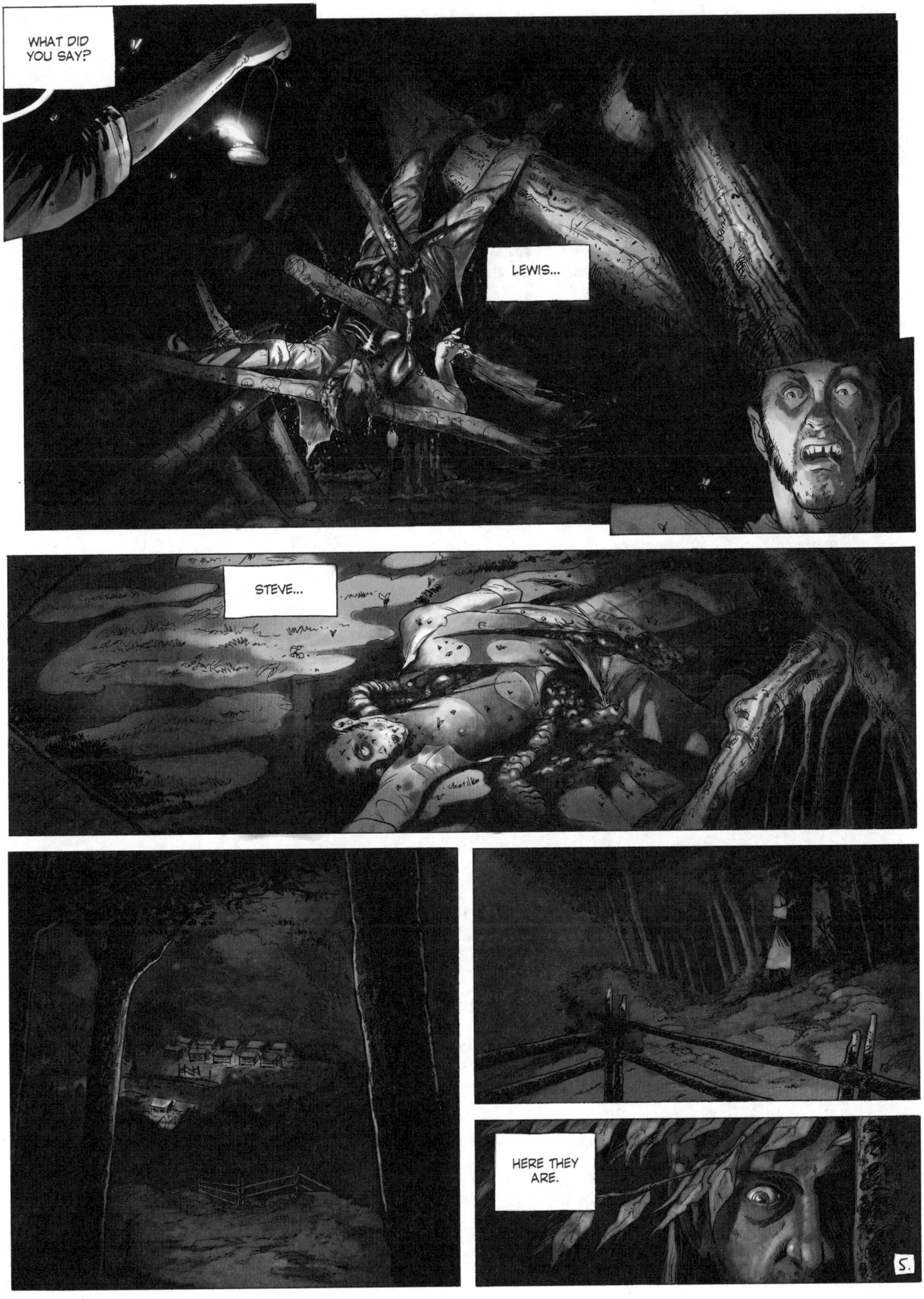
WHAT DID YOU SAY?
LEWIS...
STEVE...
HERE THEY ARE.
5.

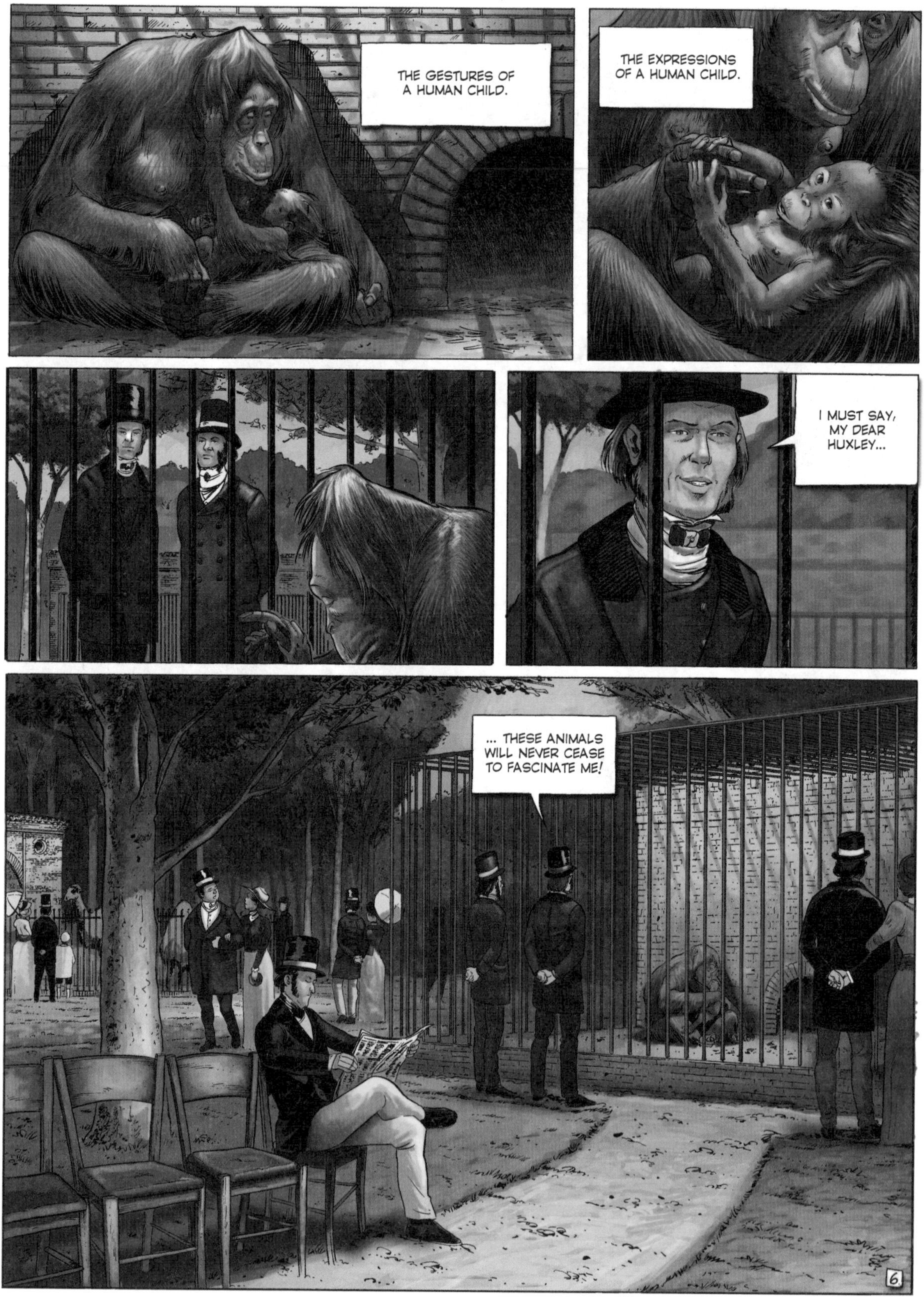
THE GESTURES OF A HUMAN CHILD.
THE EXPRESSIONS OF A HUMAN CHILD.
I MUST SAY, MY DEAR HUXLEY...
... THESE ANIMALS WILL NEVER CEASE TO FASCINATE ME!
6

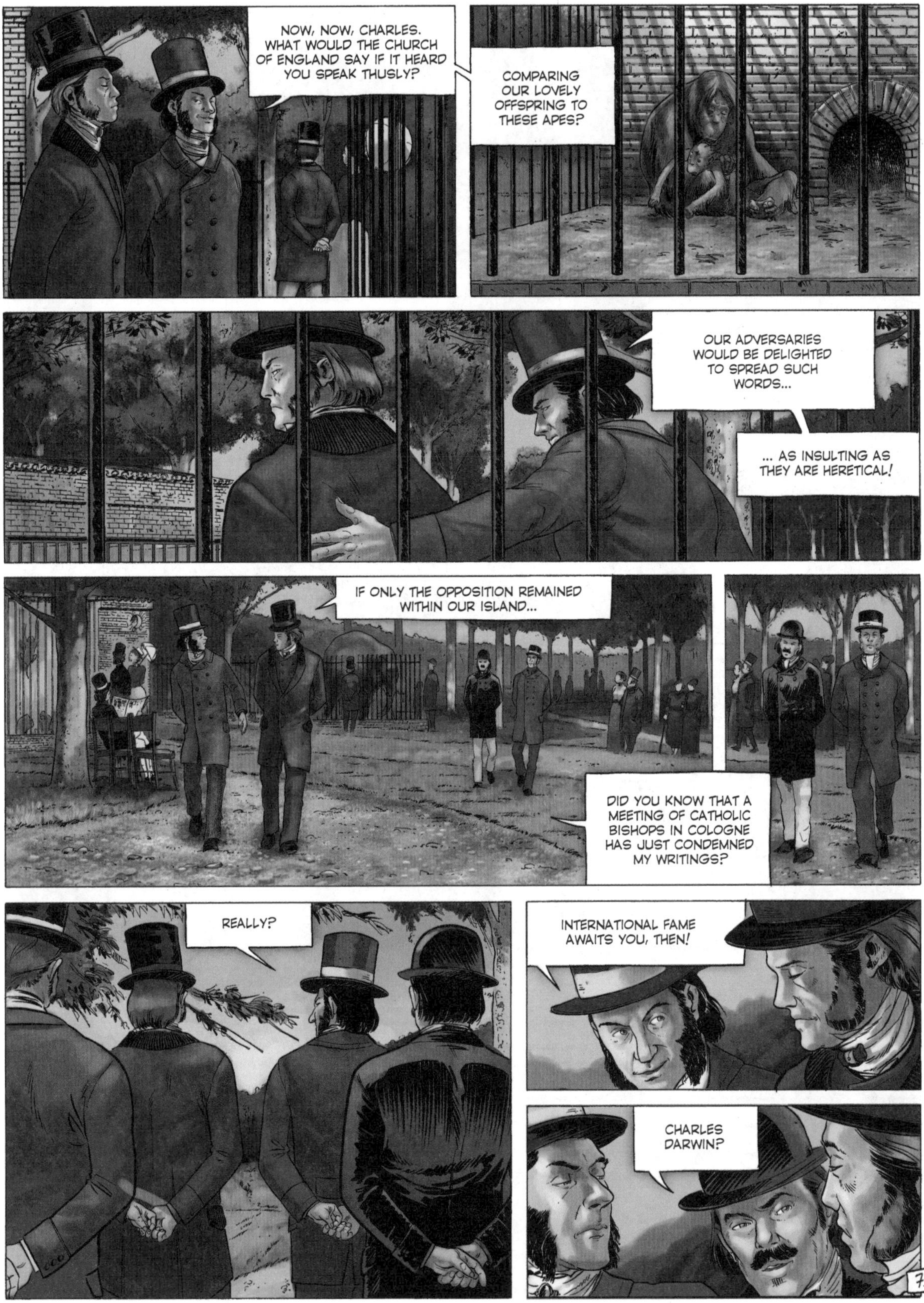
NOW, NOW, CHARLES. WHAT WOULD THE CHURCH OF ENGLAND SAY IF IT HEARD YOU SPEAK THUSLY?
COMPARING OUR LOVELY OFFSPRING TO THESE APES?
OUR ADVERSARIES WOULD BE DELIGHTED TO SPREAD SUCH WORDS...
... AS INSULTING AS THEY ARE HERETICAL!
IF ONLY THE OPPOSITION REMAINED WITHIN OUR ISLAND...
DID YOU KNOW THAT A MEETING OF CATHOLIC BISHOPS IN COLOGNE HAS JUST CONDEMNED MY WRITINGS?
REALLY?
INTERNATIONAL FAME AWAITS YOU, THEN!
CHARLES DARWIN?
7.

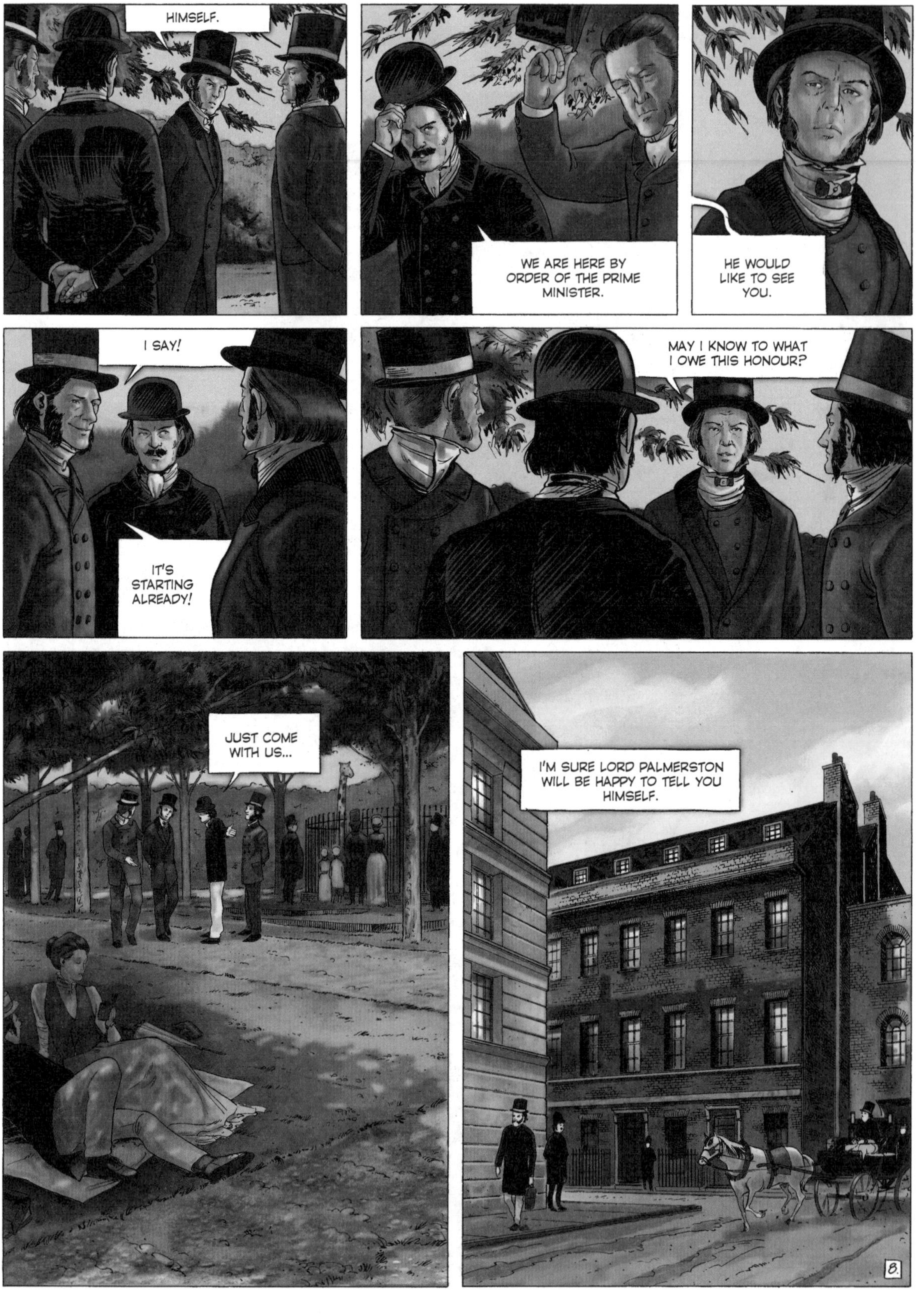
HIMSELF.
WE ARE HERE BY ORDER OF THE PRIME MINISTER.
HE WOULD LIKE TO SEE YOU.
I SAY!
IT'S STARTING ALREADY!
MAY I KNOW TO WHAT I OWE THIS HONOUR?
JUST COME WITH US...
I'M SURE LORD PALMERSTON WILL BE HAPPY TO TELL YOU HIMSELF.
8.

IMPRESSIVE.

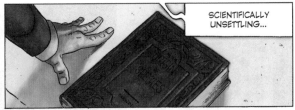

SCIENTIFICALLY UNSETTLING...

BUT INTELLECTUALLY IMPRESSIVE!

YOU SHOULD KNOW THAT I FOLLOWED YOUR EPIC JOURNEY ABOARD THE *BEAGLE* WITH GREAT ENTHUSIASM!

BECAUSE, YOU SEE...

... I'VE BEEN AN ADMIRER OF YOUR WORK FOR SOME TIME!

PRIME MINISTER, I THANK YOU FOR YOUR KIND COMPLIMENTS...

I'M TRULY FLATTERED.

BUT THIS STILL DOESN'T TELL ME WHAT I'M DOING HERE.

9.

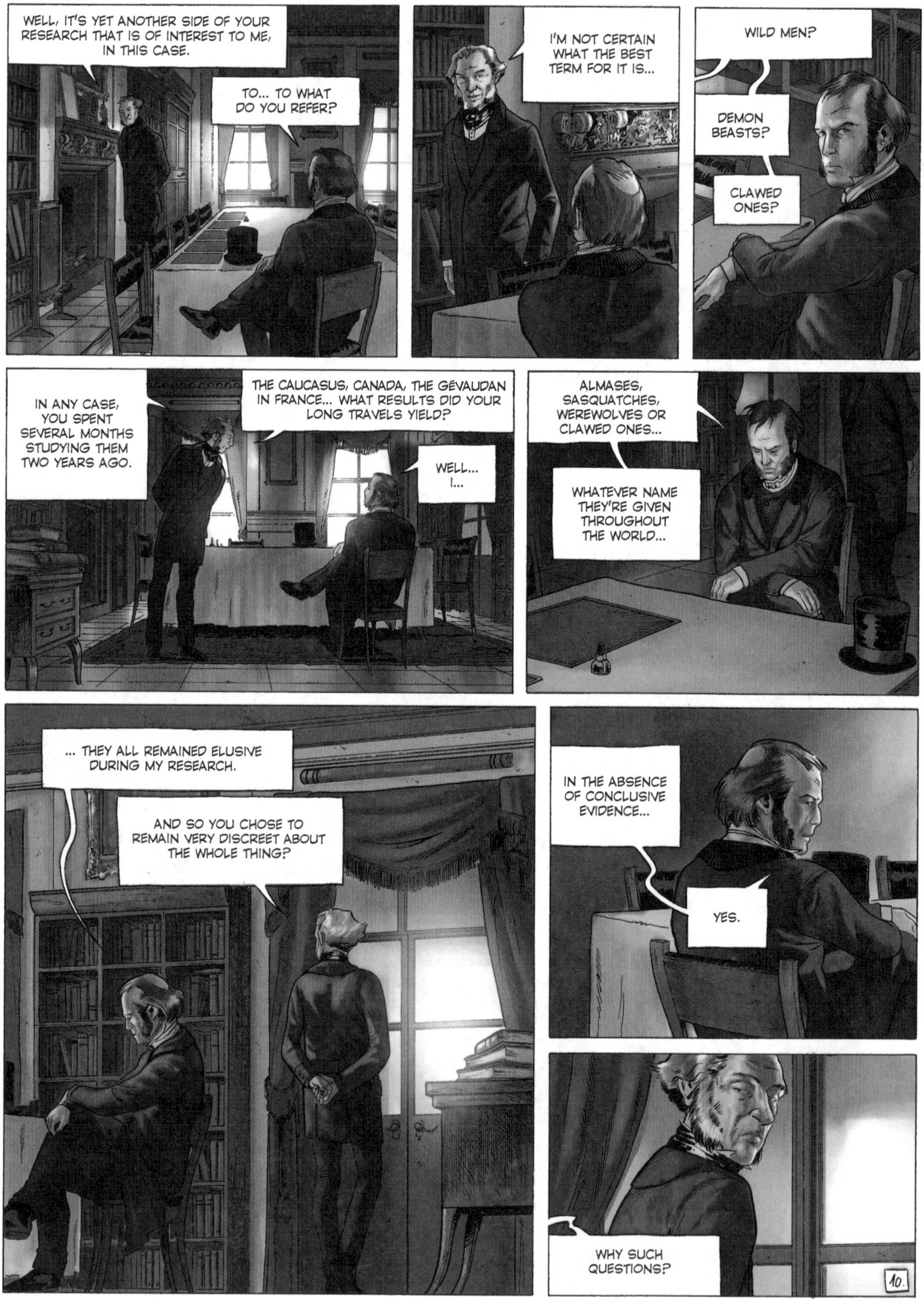
WELL, IT'S YET ANOTHER SIDE OF YOUR RESEARCH THAT IS OF INTEREST TO ME, IN THIS CASE.
TO... TO WHAT DO YOU REFER?
I'M NOT CERTAIN WHAT THE BEST TERM FOR IT IS...
WILD MEN?
DEMON BEASTS?
CLAWED ONES?
IN ANY CASE, YOU SPENT SEVERAL MONTHS STUDYING THEM TWO YEARS AGO.
THE CAUCASUS, CANADA, THE GÉVAUDAN IN FRANCE... WHAT RESULTS DID YOUR LONG TRAVELS YIELD?
WELL... I...
ALMASES, SASQUATCHES, WEREWOLVES OR CLAWED ONES...
WHATEVER NAME THEY'RE GIVEN THROUGHOUT THE WORLD...
... THEY ALL REMAINED ELUSIVE DURING MY RESEARCH.
AND SO YOU CHOSE TO REMAIN VERY DISCREET ABOUT THE WHOLE THING?
IN THE ABSENCE OF CONCLUSIVE EVIDENCE...
YES.
WHY SUCH QUESTIONS?
10.

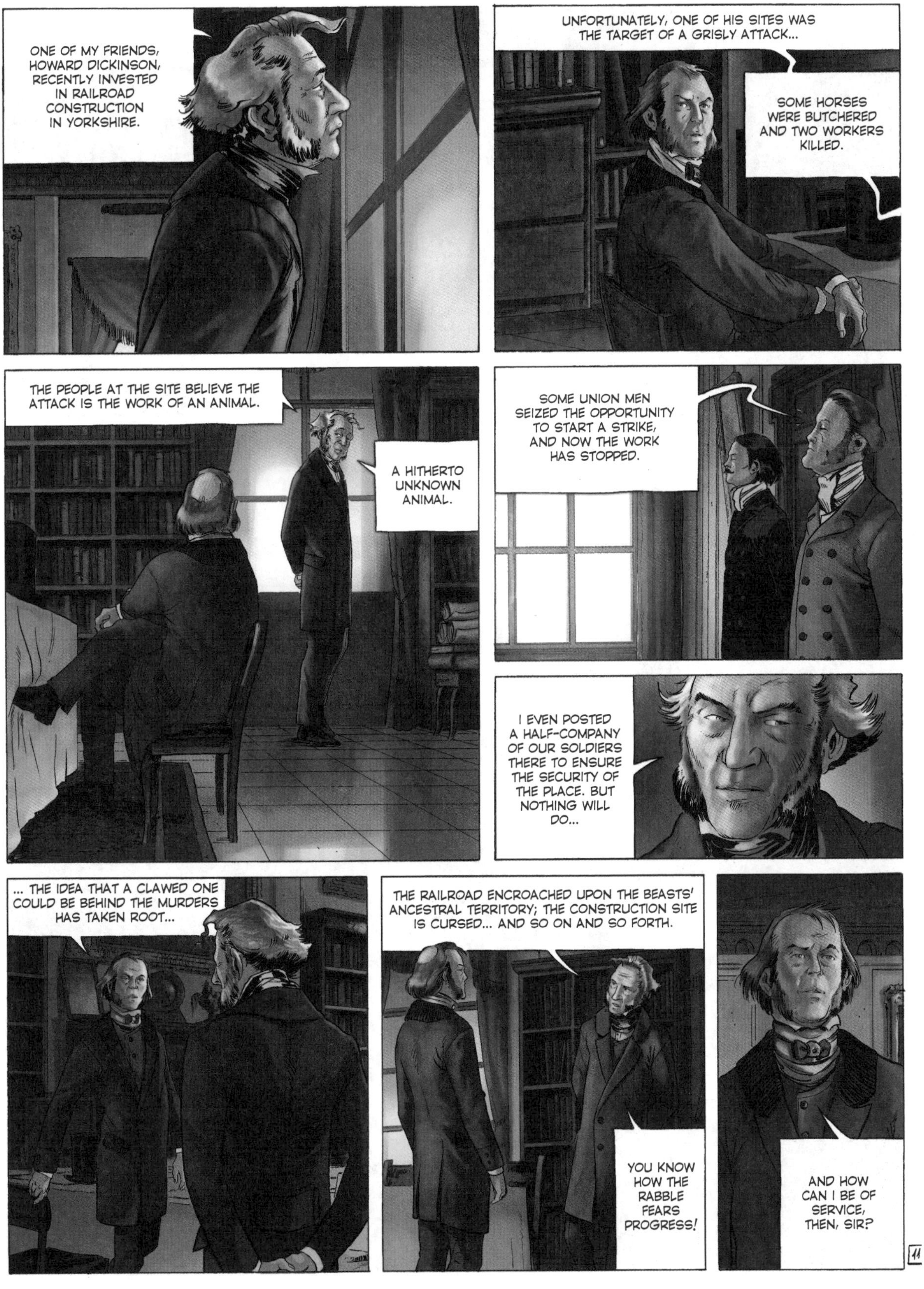
ONE OF MY FRIENDS, HOWARD DICKINSON, RECENTLY INVESTED IN RAILROAD CONSTRUCTION IN YORKSHIRE.
UNFORTUNATELY, ONE OF HIS SITES WAS THE TARGET OF A GRISLY ATTACK...
SOME HORSES WERE BUTCHERED AND TWO WORKERS KILLED.
THE PEOPLE AT THE SITE BELIEVE THE ATTACK IS THE WORK OF AN ANIMAL.
A HITHERTO UNKNOWN ANIMAL.
SOME UNION MEN SEIZED THE OPPORTUNITY TO START A STRIKE, AND NOW THE WORK HAS STOPPED.
I EVEN POSTED A HALF-COMPANY OF OUR SOLDIERS THERE TO ENSURE THE SECURITY OF THE PLACE. BUT NOTHING WILL DO...
... THE IDEA THAT A CLAWED ONE COULD BE BEHIND THE MURDERS HAS TAKEN ROOT...
THE RAILROAD ENCROACHED UPON THE BEASTS' ANCESTRAL TERRITORY; THE CONSTRUCTION SITE IS CURSED... AND SO ON AND SO FORTH.
YOU KNOW HOW THE RABBLE FEARS PROGRESS!
AND HOW CAN I BE OF SERVICE, THEN, SIR?
11

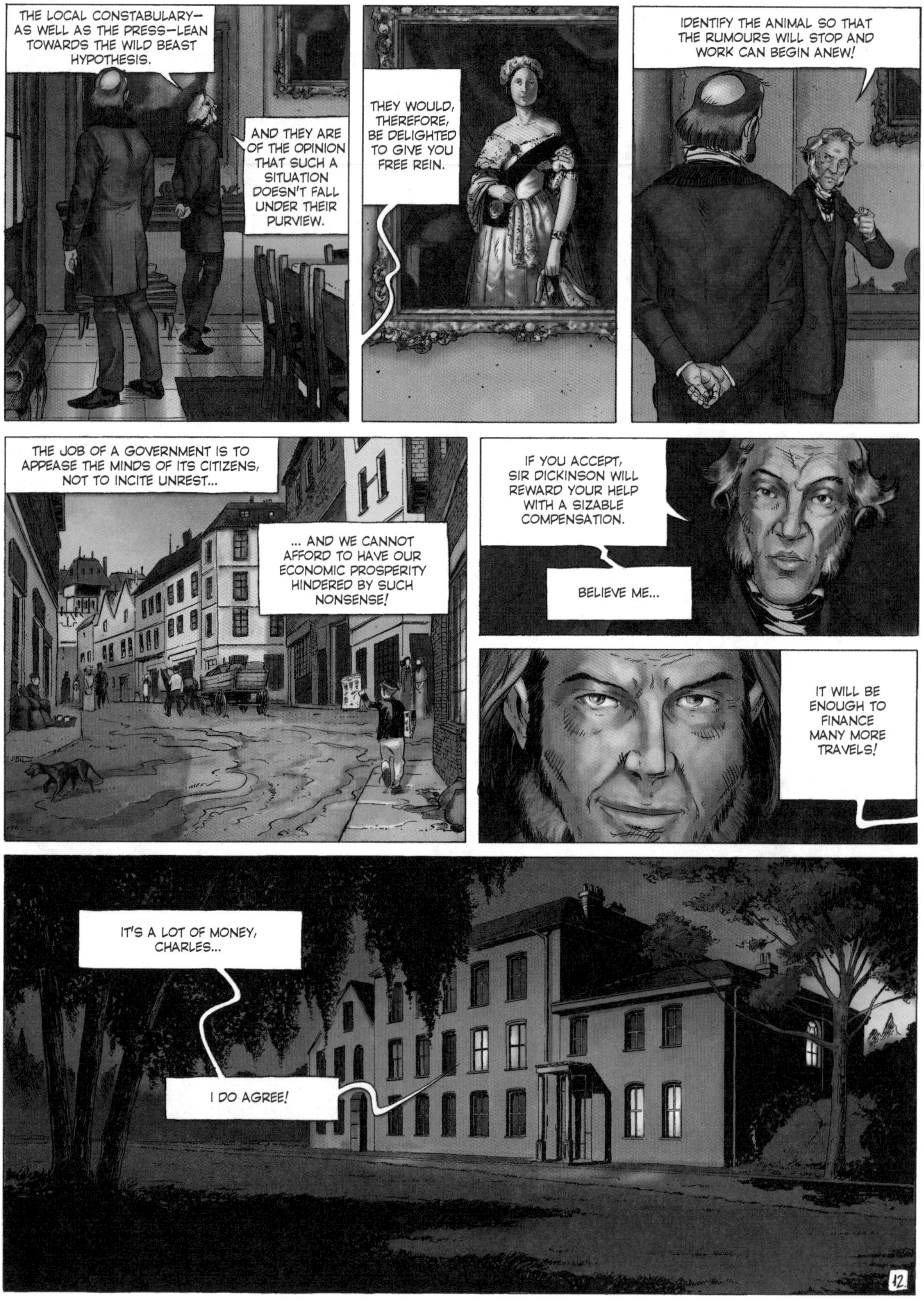
THE LOCAL CONSTABULARY—AS WELL AS THE PRESS—LEAN TOWARDS THE WILD BEAST HYPOTHESIS.
AND THEY ARE OF THE OPINION THAT SUCH A SITUATION DOESN'T FALL UNDER THEIR PURVIEW.
THEY WOULD, THEREFORE, BE DELIGHTED TO GIVE YOU FREE REIN.
IDENTIFY THE ANIMAL SO THAT THE RUMOURS WILL STOP AND WORK CAN BEGIN ANEW!
THE JOB OF A GOVERNMENT IS TO APPEASE THE MINDS OF ITS CITIZENS, NOT TO INCITE UNREST...
... AND WE CANNOT AFFORD TO HAVE OUR ECONOMIC PROSPERITY HINDERED BY SUCH NONSENSE!
IF YOU ACCEPT, SIR DICKINSON WILL REWARD YOUR HELP WITH A SIZABLE COMPENSATION.
BELIEVE ME...
IT WILL BE ENOUGH TO FINANCE MANY MORE TRAVELS!
IT'S A LOT OF MONEY, CHARLES...
I DO AGREE!
12

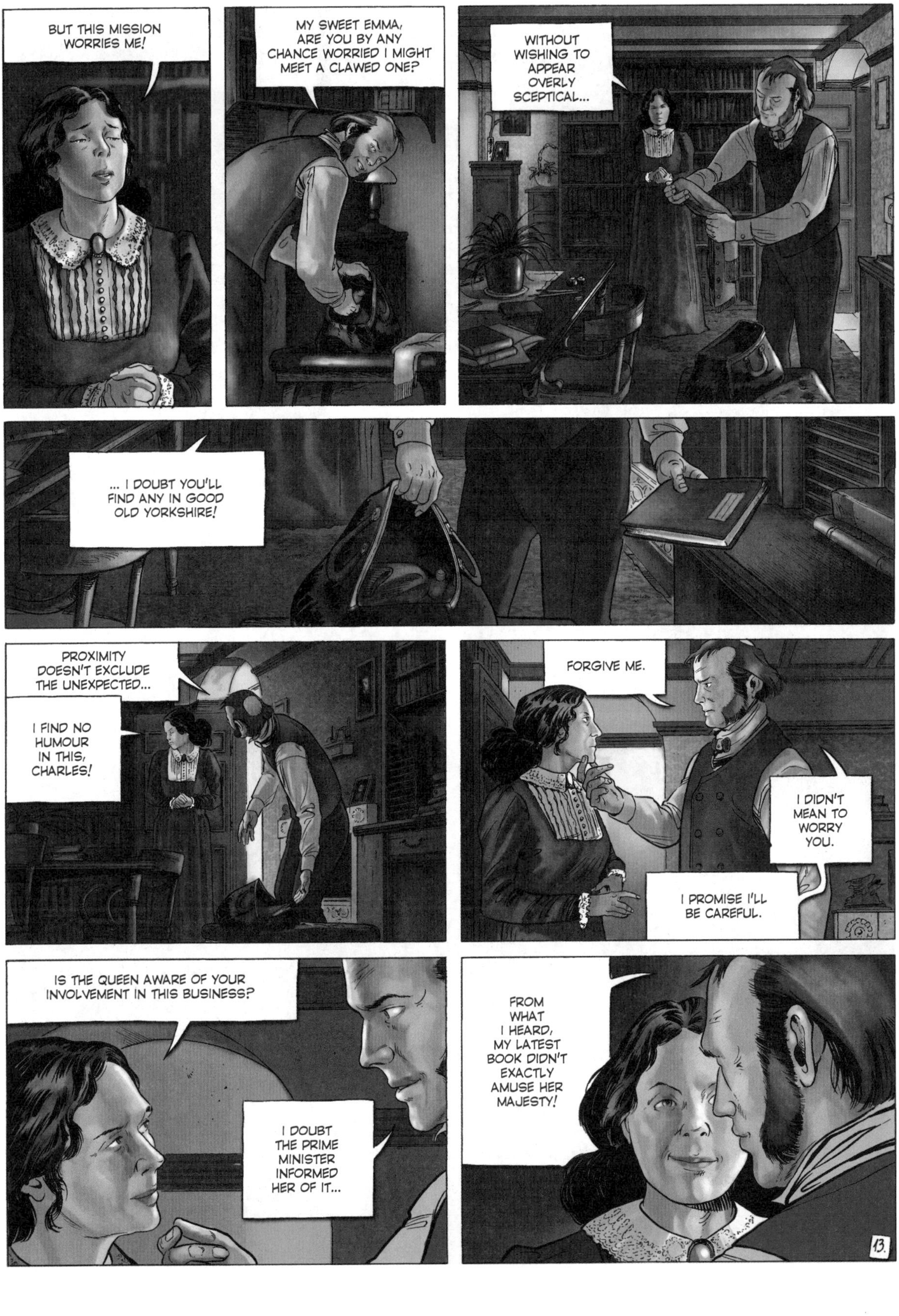
BUT THIS MISSION WORRIES ME!
MY SWEET EMMA, ARE YOU BY ANY CHANCE WORRIED I MIGHT MEET A CLAWED ONE?
WITHOUT WISHING TO APPEAR OVERLY SCEPTICAL...
... I DOUBT YOU'LL FIND ANY IN GOOD OLD YORKSHIRE!
PROXIMITY DOESN'T EXCLUDE THE UNEXPECTED...
I FIND NO HUMOUR IN THIS, CHARLES!
FORGIVE ME.
I DIDN'T MEAN TO WORRY YOU.
I PROMISE I'LL BE CAREFUL.
IS THE QUEEN AWARE OF YOUR INVOLVEMENT IN THIS BUSINESS?
I DOUBT THE PRIME MINISTER INFORMED HER OF IT...
FROM WHAT I HEARD, MY LATEST BOOK DIDN'T EXACTLY AMUSE HER MAJESTY!
13.

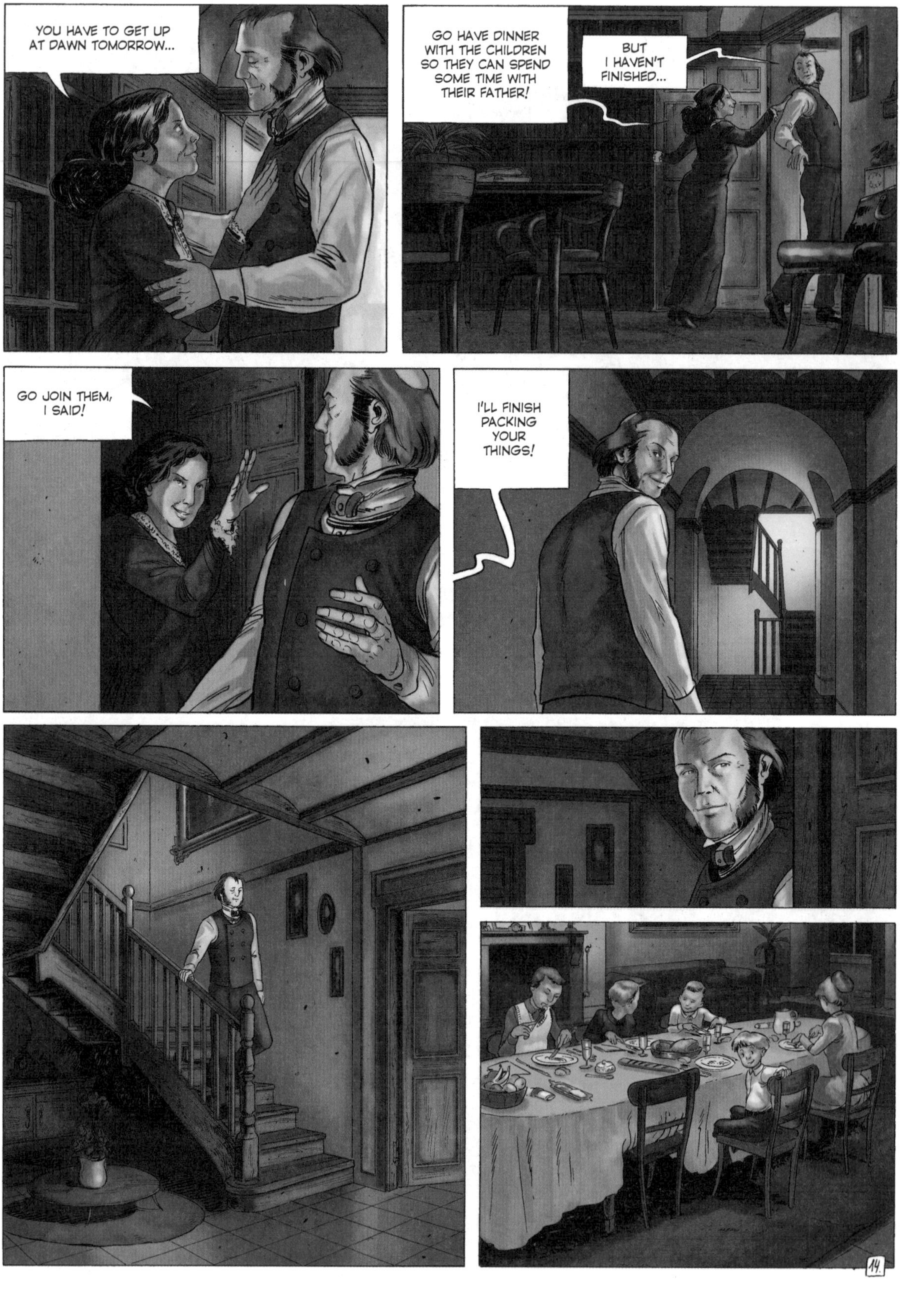
YOU HAVE TO GET UP AT DAWN TOMORROW...
GO HAVE DINNER WITH THE CHILDREN SO THEY CAN SPEND SOME TIME WITH THEIR FATHER!
BUT I HAVEN'T FINISHED...
GO JOIN THEM, I SAID!
I'LL FINISH PACKING YOUR THINGS!
14.

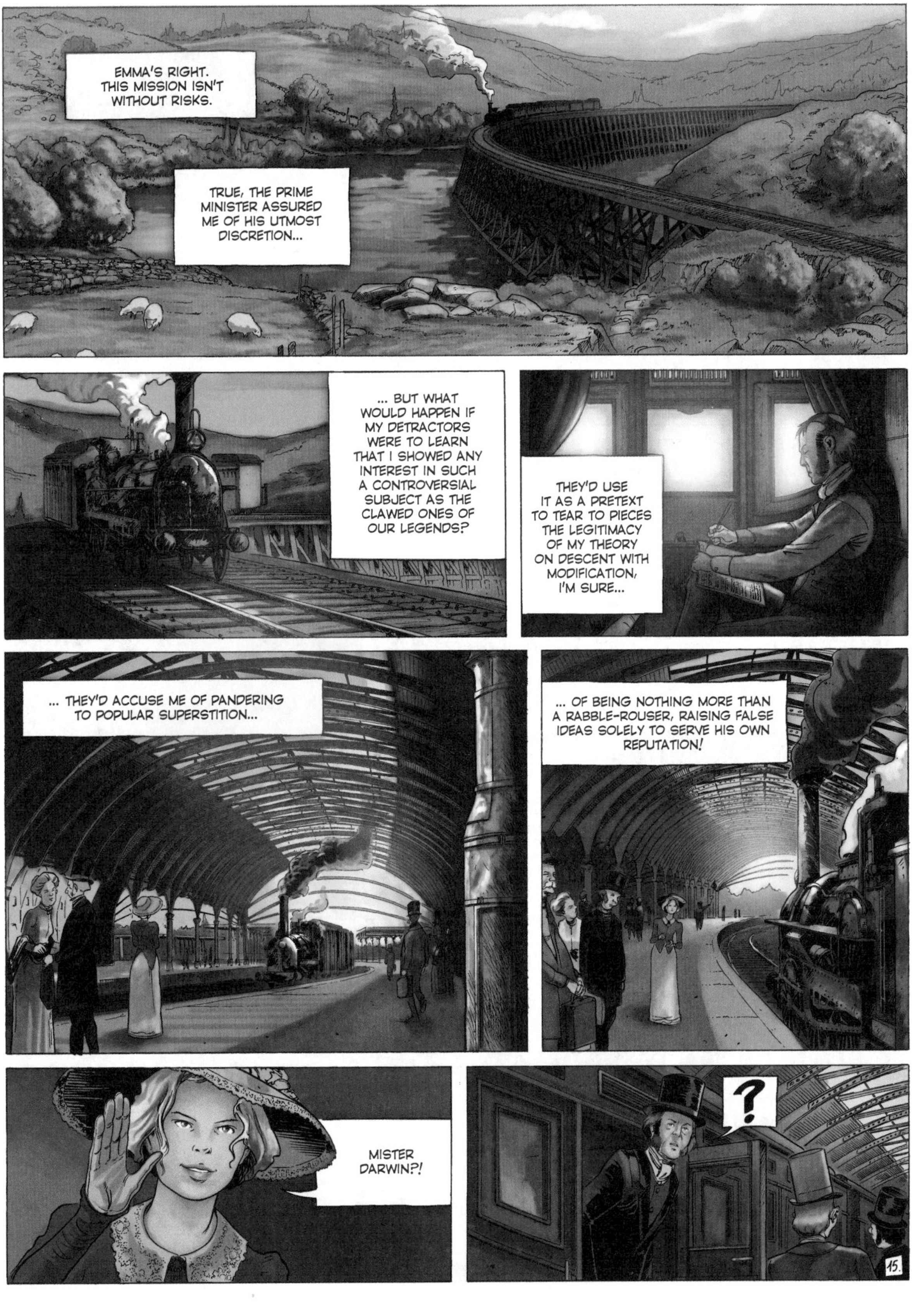
EMMA'S RIGHT. THIS MISSION ISN'T WITHOUT RISKS.
TRUE, THE PRIME MINISTER ASSURED ME OF HIS UTMOST DISCRETION...
... BUT WHAT WOULD HAPPEN IF MY DETRACTORS WERE TO LEARN THAT I SHOWED ANY INTEREST IN SUCH A CONTROVERSIAL SUBJECT AS THE CLAWED ONES OF OUR LEGENDS?
THEY'D USE IT AS A PRETEXT TO TEAR TO PIECES THE LEGITIMACY OF MY THEORY ON DESCENT WITH MODIFICATION, I'M SURE...
... THEY'D ACCUSE ME OF PANDERING TO POPULAR SUPERSTITION...
... OF BEING NOTHING MORE THAN A RABBLE-ROUSER, RAISING FALSE IDEAS SOLELY TO SERVE HIS OWN REPUTATION!
MISTER DARWIN?!
?
15.

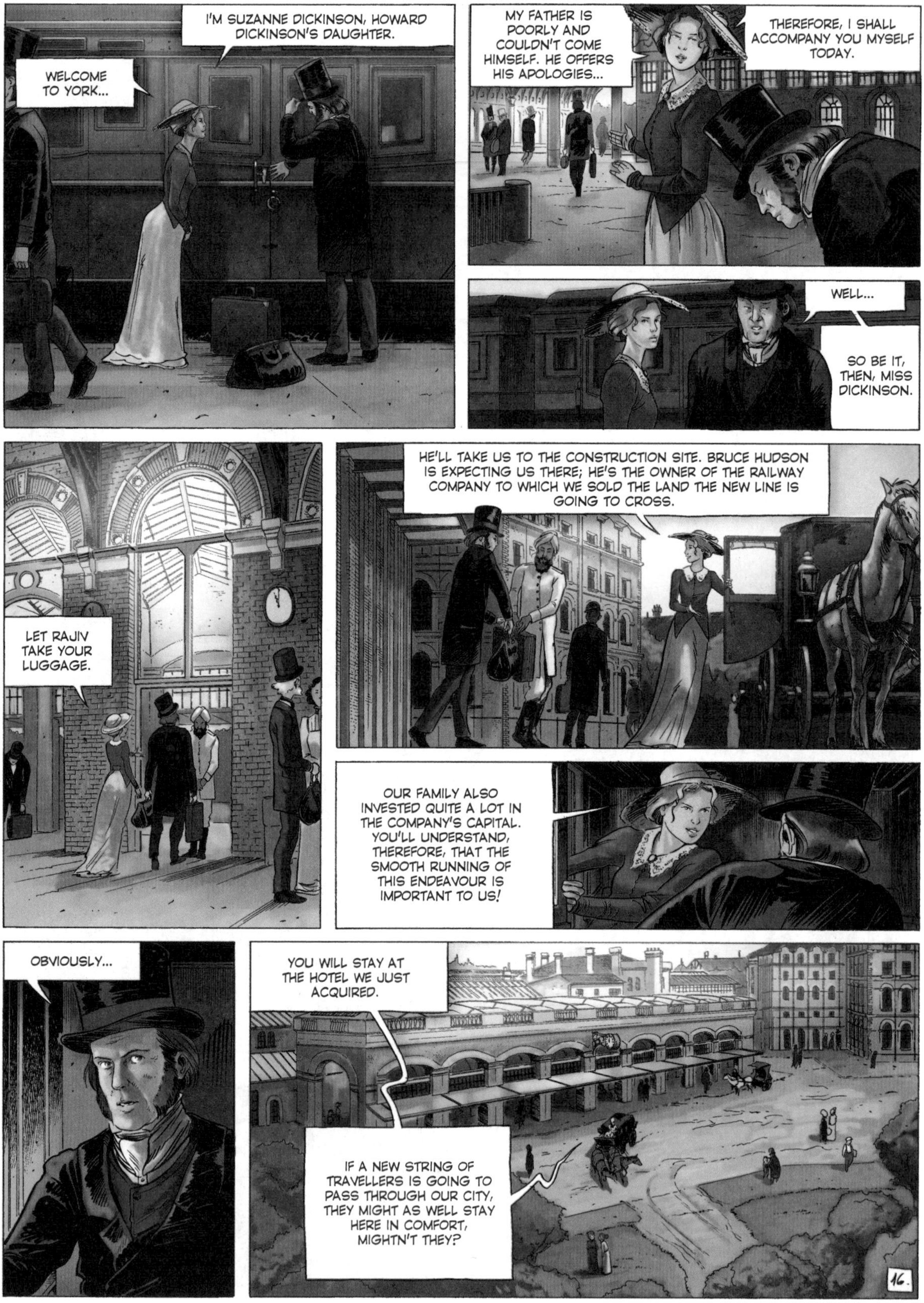
I'M SUZANNE DICKINSON, HOWARD DICKINSON'S DAUGHTER.
WELCOME TO YORK...
MY FATHER IS POORLY AND COULDN'T COME HIMSELF. HE OFFERS HIS APOLOGIES...
THEREFORE, I SHALL ACCOMPANY YOU MYSELF TODAY.
WELL...
SO BE IT, THEN, MISS DICKINSON.
LET RAJIV TAKE YOUR LUGGAGE.
HE'LL TAKE US TO THE CONSTRUCTION SITE. BRUCE HUDSON IS EXPECTING US THERE; HE'S THE OWNER OF THE RAILWAY COMPANY TO WHICH WE SOLD THE LAND THE NEW LINE IS GOING TO CROSS.
OUR FAMILY ALSO INVESTED QUITE A LOT IN THE COMPANY'S CAPITAL. YOU'LL UNDERSTAND, THEREFORE, THAT THE SMOOTH RUNNING OF THIS ENDEAVOUR IS IMPORTANT TO US!
OBVIOUSLY...
YOU WILL STAY AT THE HOTEL WE JUST ACQUIRED.
IF A NEW STRING OF TRAVELLERS IS GOING TO PASS THROUGH OUR CITY, THEY MIGHT AS WELL STAY HERE IN COMFORT, MIGHTN'T THEY?
16.

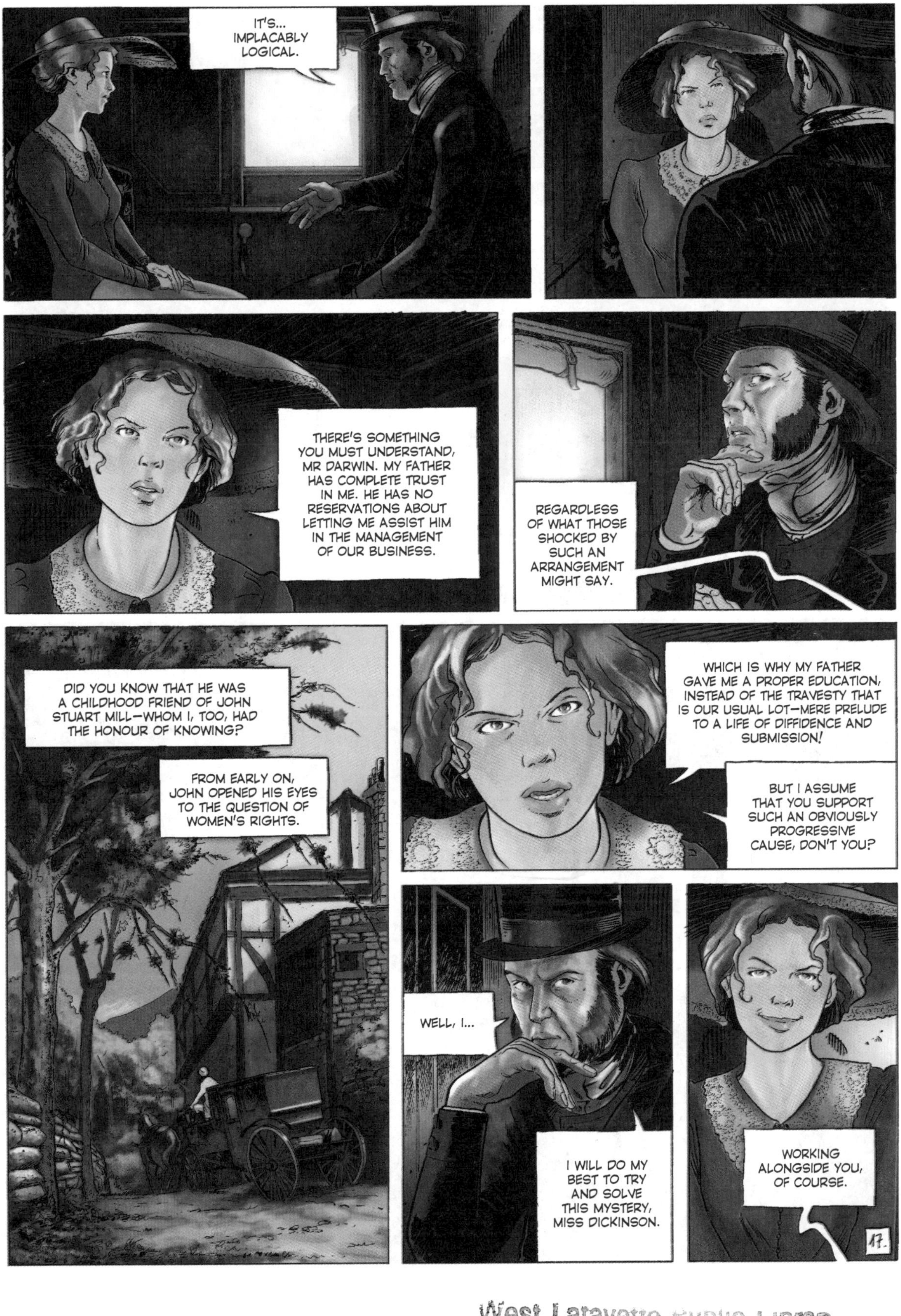
IT'S... IMPLACABLY LOGICAL.
THERE'S SOMETHING YOU MUST UNDERSTAND, MR DARWIN. MY FATHER HAS COMPLETE TRUST IN ME. HE HAS NO RESERVATIONS ABOUT LETTING ME ASSIST HIM IN THE MANAGEMENT OF OUR BUSINESS.
REGARDLESS OF WHAT THOSE SHOCKED BY SUCH AN ARRANGEMENT MIGHT SAY.
DID YOU KNOW THAT HE WAS A CHILDHOOD FRIEND OF JOHN STUART MILL—WHOM I, TOO, HAD THE HONOUR OF KNOWING?
FROM EARLY ON, JOHN OPENED HIS EYES TO THE QUESTION OF WOMEN'S RIGHTS.
WHICH IS WHY MY FATHER GAVE ME A PROPER EDUCATION, INSTEAD OF THE TRAVESTY THAT IS OUR USUAL LOT—MERE PRELUDE TO A LIFE OF DIFFIDENCE AND SUBMISSION!
BUT I ASSUME THAT YOU SUPPORT SUCH AN OBVIOUSLY PROGRESSIVE CAUSE, DON'T YOU?
WELL, I...
I WILL DO MY BEST TO TRY AND SOLVE THIS MYSTERY, MISS DICKINSON.
WORKING ALONGSIDE YOU, OF COURSE.
17.

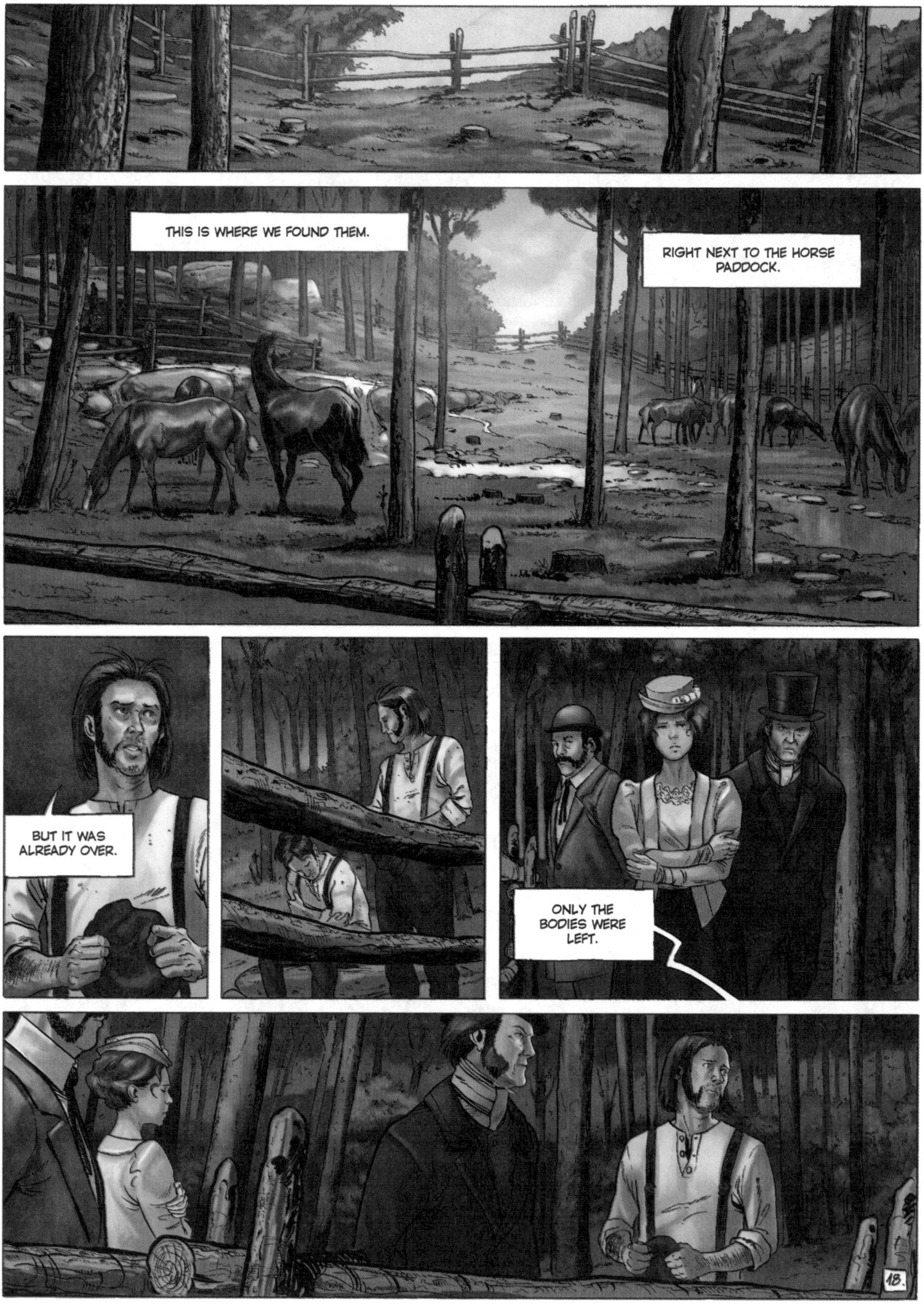
THIS IS WHERE WE FOUND THEM.
RIGHT NEXT TO THE HORSE PADDOCK.
BUT IT WAS ALREADY OVER.
ONLY THE BODIES WERE LEFT.
18.

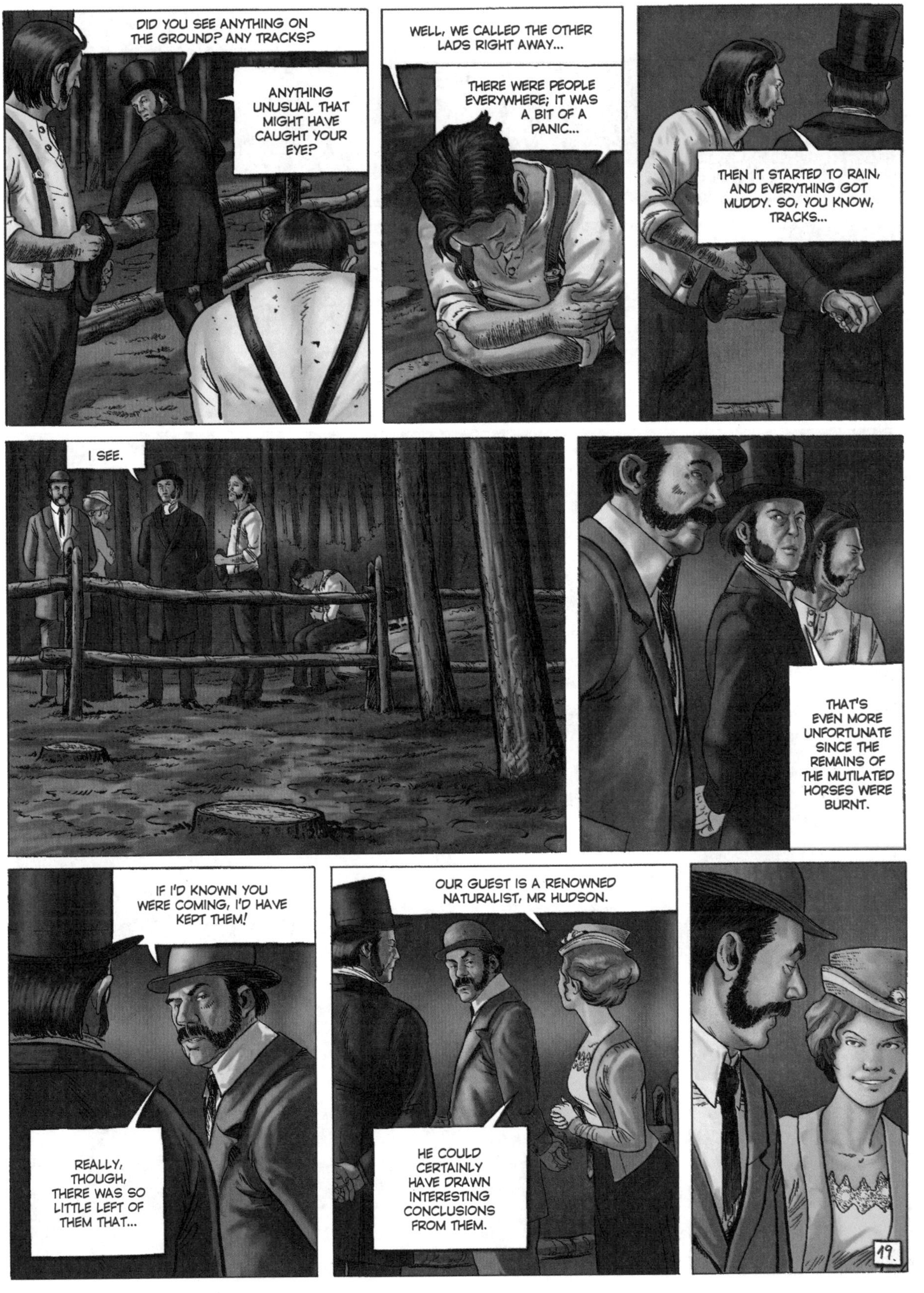
DID YOU SEE ANYTHING ON THE GROUND? ANY TRACKS?
ANYTHING UNUSUAL THAT MIGHT HAVE CAUGHT YOUR EYE?
WELL, WE CALLED THE OTHER LADS RIGHT AWAY...
THERE WERE PEOPLE EVERYWHERE; IT WAS A BIT OF A PANIC...
THEN IT STARTED TO RAIN, AND EVERYTHING GOT MUDDY. SO, YOU KNOW, TRACKS...
I SEE.
THAT'S EVEN MORE UNFORTUNATE SINCE THE REMAINS OF THE MUTILATED HORSES WERE BURNT.
IF I'D KNOWN YOU WERE COMING, I'D HAVE KEPT THEM!
REALLY, THOUGH, THERE WAS SO LITTLE LEFT OF THEM THAT...
OUR GUEST IS A RENOWNED NATURALIST, MR HUDSON.
HE COULD CERTAINLY HAVE DRAWN INTERESTING CONCLUSIONS FROM THEM.
19.

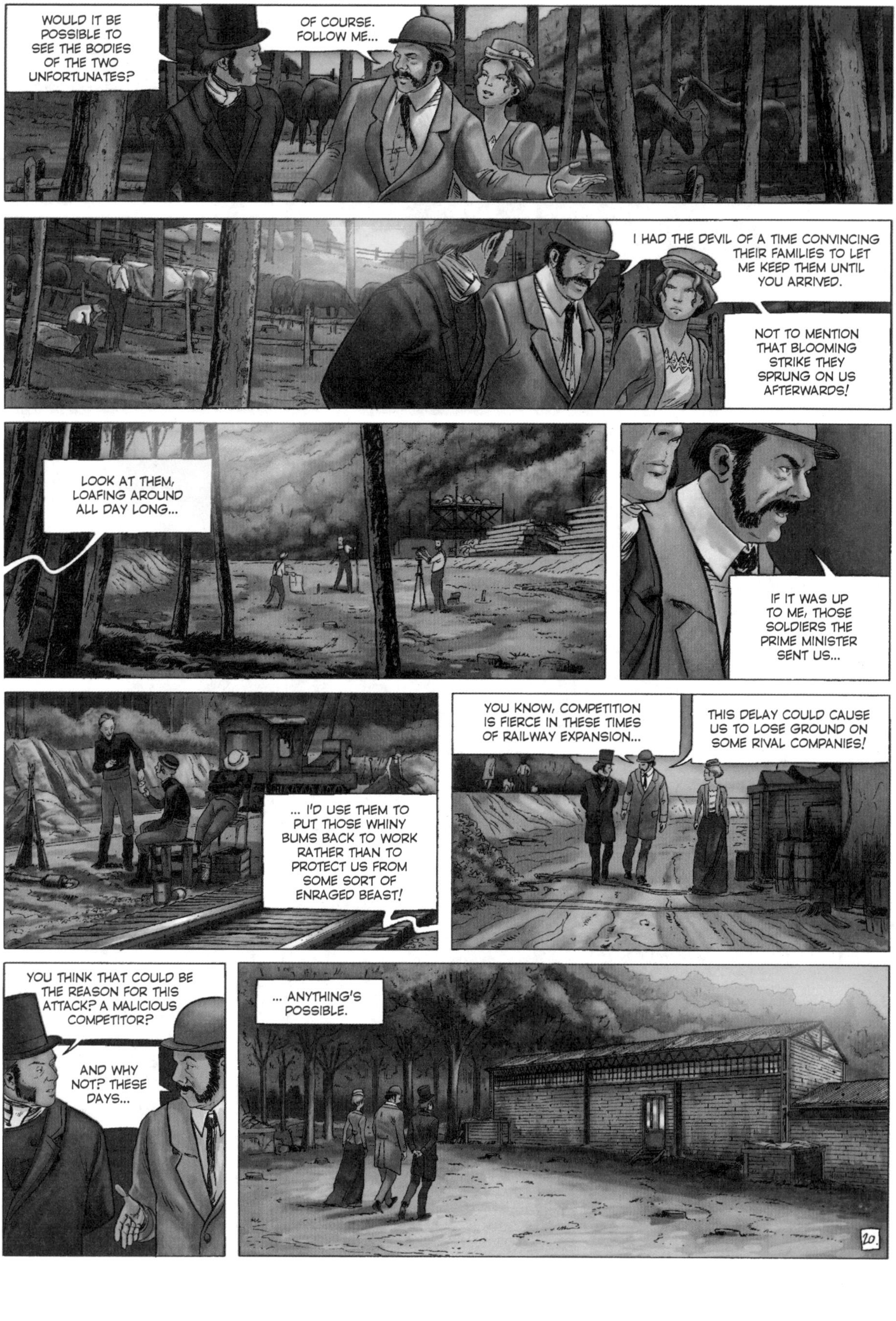
WOULD IT BE POSSIBLE TO SEE THE BODIES OF THE TWO UNFORTUNATES?
OF COURSE. FOLLOW ME...
I HAD THE DEVIL OF A TIME CONVINCING THEIR FAMILIES TO LET ME KEEP THEM UNTIL YOU ARRIVED.
NOT TO MENTION THAT BLOOMING STRIKE THEY SPRUNG ON US AFTERWARDS!
LOOK AT THEM, LOAFING AROUND ALL DAY LONG...
IF IT WAS UP TO ME, THOSE SOLDIERS THE PRIME MINISTER SENT US...
... I'D USE THEM TO PUT THOSE WHINY BUMS BACK TO WORK RATHER THAN TO PROTECT US FROM SOME SORT OF ENRAGED BEAST!
YOU KNOW, COMPETITION IS FIERCE IN THESE TIMES OF RAILWAY EXPANSION...
THIS DELAY COULD CAUSE US TO LOSE GROUND ON SOME RIVAL COMPANIES!
YOU THINK THAT COULD BE THE REASON FOR THIS ATTACK? A MALICIOUS COMPETITOR?
AND WHY NOT? THESE DAYS...
... ANYTHING'S POSSIBLE.
20.

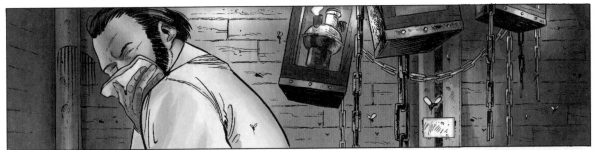

DEEP PERFORATION OF THE CHEST...

THAT... THAT'S THE ONE WE FOUND IMPALED ON THE FENCE.

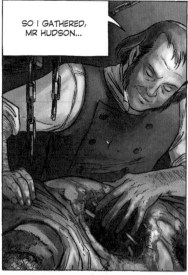

SO I GATHERED, MR HUDSON...

WHAT I'M WONDERING IS HOW A MAN THAT SIZE COULD HAVE BEEN THROWN THUS ONTO THE FENCE?

AND HERE, ON HIS SIDE: IT LOOKS LIKE CLAW MARKS— REALLY LARGE ONES...

THEY BIT DEEP INTO THE FLESH AND SNAPPED THE BONES.

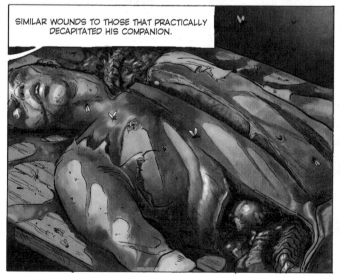

SIMILAR WOUNDS TO THOSE THAT PRACTICALLY DECAPITATED HIS COMPANION.

THESE TWO MEN MUST HAVE DIED INSTANTLY...

22

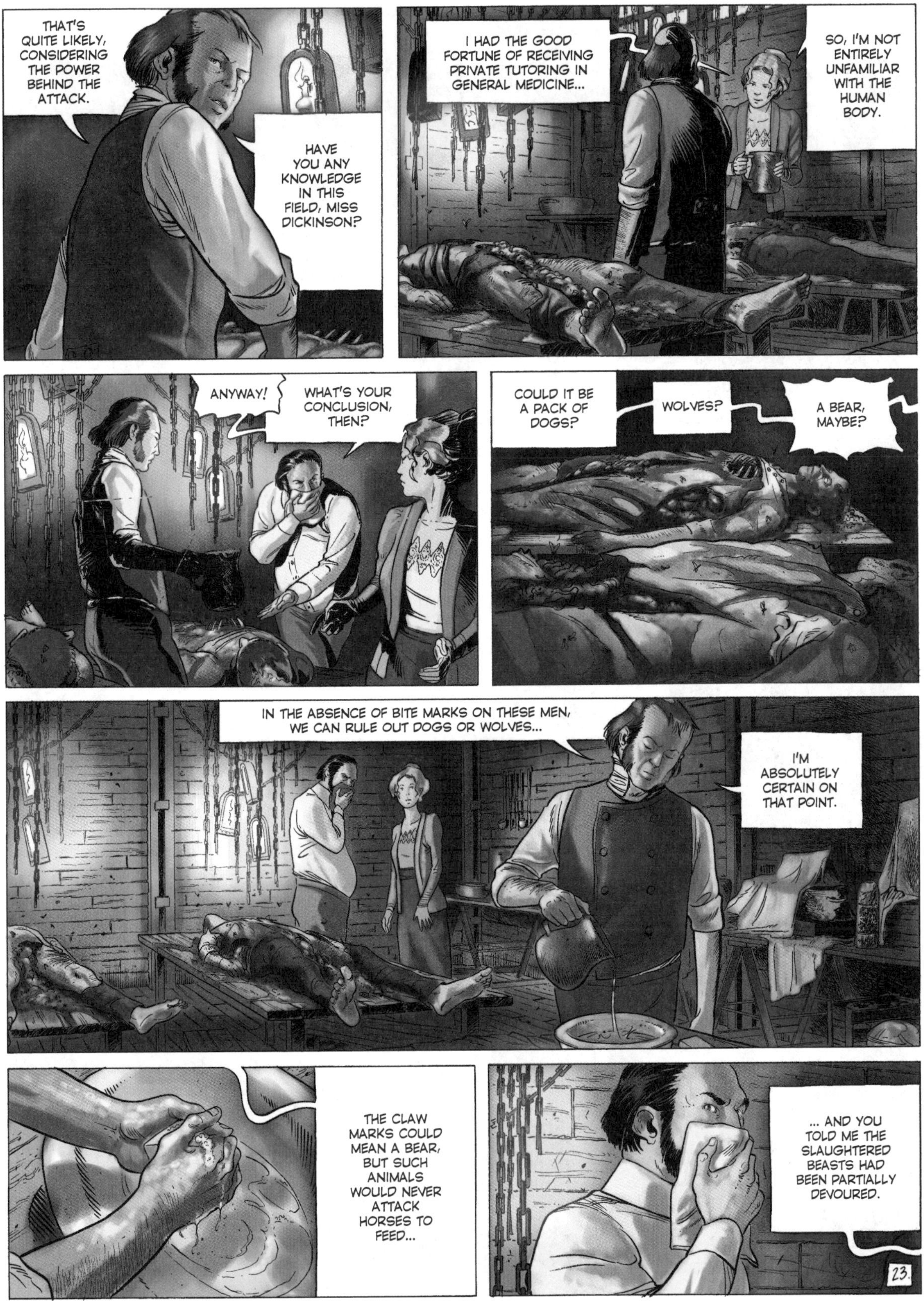
THAT'S QUITE LIKELY, CONSIDERING THE POWER BEHIND THE ATTACK.
HAVE YOU ANY KNOWLEDGE IN THIS FIELD, MISS DICKINSON?
I HAD THE GOOD FORTUNE OF RECEIVING PRIVATE TUTORING IN GENERAL MEDICINE...
SO, I'M NOT ENTIRELY UNFAMILIAR WITH THE HUMAN BODY.
ANYWAY!
WHAT'S YOUR CONCLUSION, THEN?
COULD IT BE A PACK OF DOGS?
WOLVES?
A BEAR, MAYBE?
IN THE ABSENCE OF BITE MARKS ON THESE MEN, WE CAN RULE OUT DOGS OR WOLVES...
I'M ABSOLUTELY CERTAIN ON THAT POINT.
THE CLAW MARKS COULD MEAN A BEAR, BUT SUCH ANIMALS WOULD NEVER ATTACK HORSES TO FEED...
... AND YOU TOLD ME THE SLAUGHTERED BEASTS HAD BEEN PARTIALLY DEVOURED.
23.

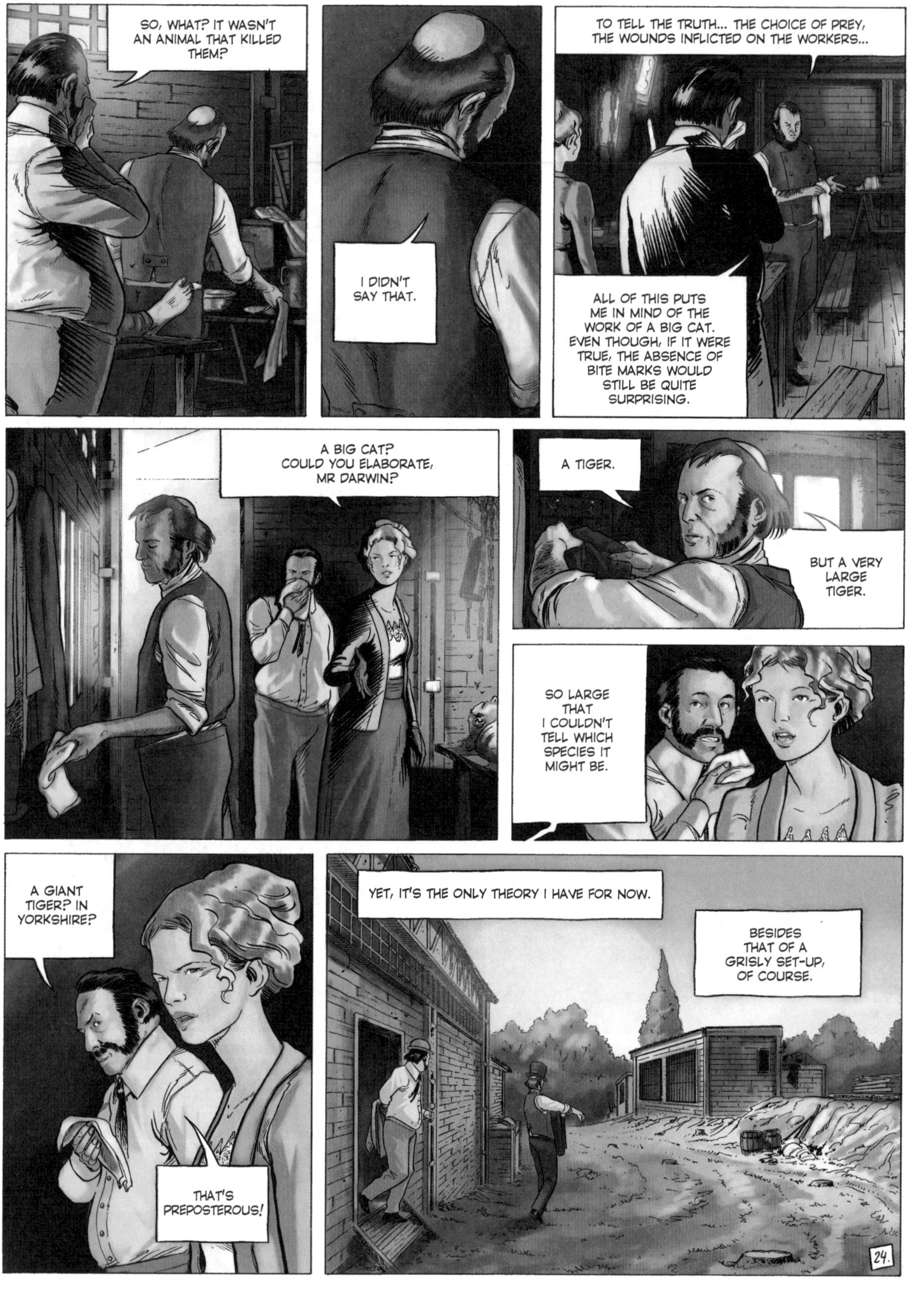
SO, WHAT? IT WASN'T AN ANIMAL THAT KILLED THEM?
I DIDN'T SAY THAT.
TO TELL THE TRUTH... THE CHOICE OF PREY, THE WOUNDS INFLICTED ON THE WORKERS...
ALL OF THIS PUTS ME IN MIND OF THE WORK OF A BIG CAT. EVEN THOUGH, IF IT WERE TRUE, THE ABSENCE OF BITE MARKS WOULD STILL BE QUITE SURPRISING.
A BIG CAT? COULD YOU ELABORATE, MR DARWIN?
A TIGER.
BUT A VERY LARGE TIGER.
SO LARGE THAT I COULDN'T TELL WHICH SPECIES IT MIGHT BE.
A GIANT TIGER? IN YORKSHIRE?
THAT'S PREPOSTEROUS!
YET, IT'S THE ONLY THEORY I HAVE FOR NOW.
BESIDES THAT OF A GRISLY SET-UP, OF COURSE.
24.

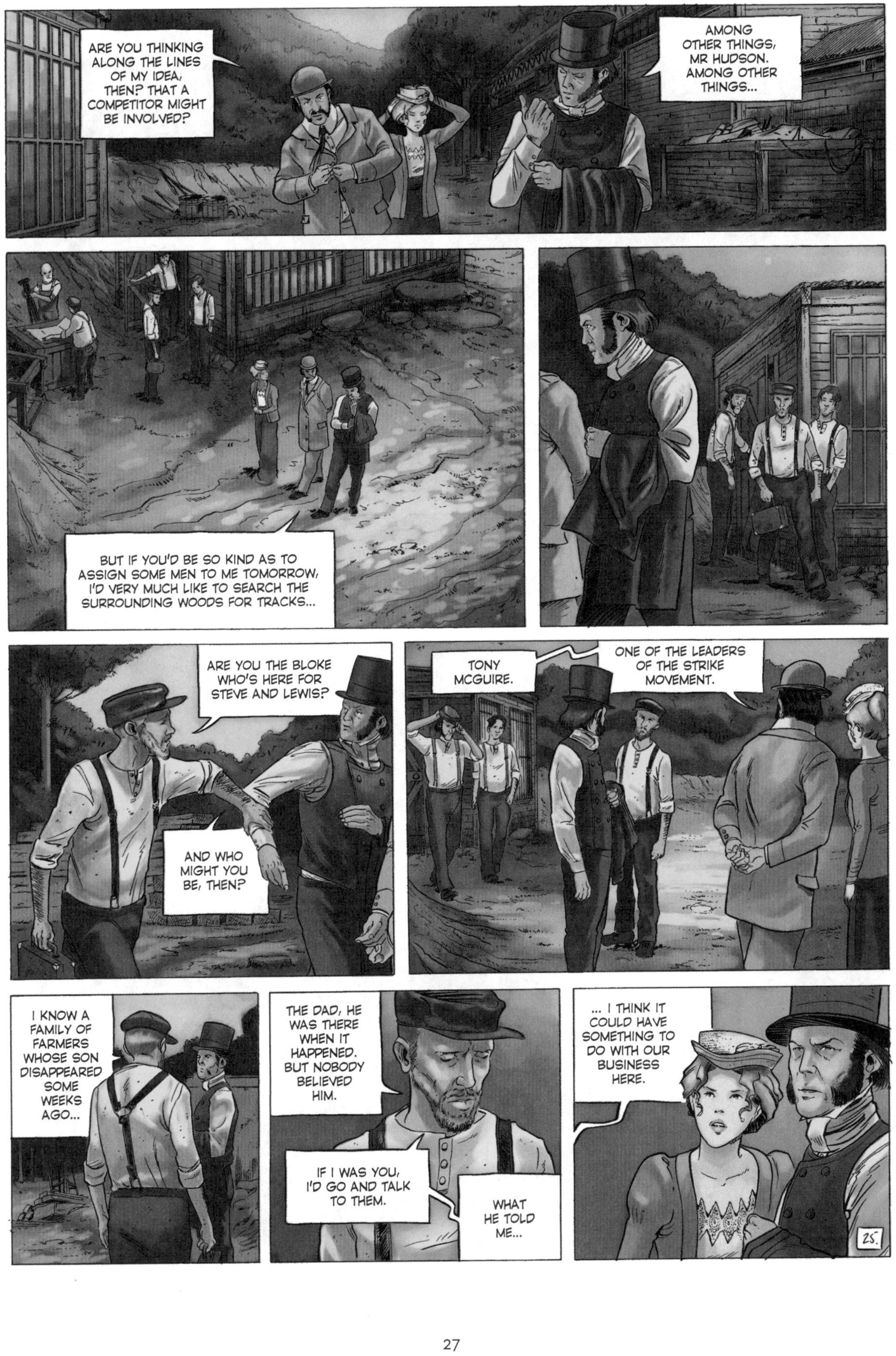
ARE YOU THINKING ALONG THE LINES OF MY IDEA, THEN? THAT A COMPETITOR MIGHT BE INVOLVED?
AMONG OTHER THINGS, MR HUDSON. AMONG OTHER THINGS...
BUT IF YOU'D BE SO KIND AS TO ASSIGN SOME MEN TO ME TOMORROW, I'D VERY MUCH LIKE TO SEARCH THE SURROUNDING WOODS FOR TRACKS...
ARE YOU THE BLOKE WHO'S HERE FOR STEVE AND LEWIS?
AND WHO MIGHT YOU BE, THEN?
TONY MCGUIRE.
ONE OF THE LEADERS OF THE STRIKE MOVEMENT.
I KNOW A FAMILY OF FARMERS WHOSE SON DISAPPEARED SOME WEEKS AGO...
THE DAD, HE WAS THERE WHEN IT HAPPENED. BUT NOBODY BELIEVED HIM.
IF I WAS YOU, I'D GO AND TALK TO THEM.
WHAT HE TOLD ME...
... I THINK IT COULD HAVE SOMETHING TO DO WITH OUR BUSINESS HERE.
25.

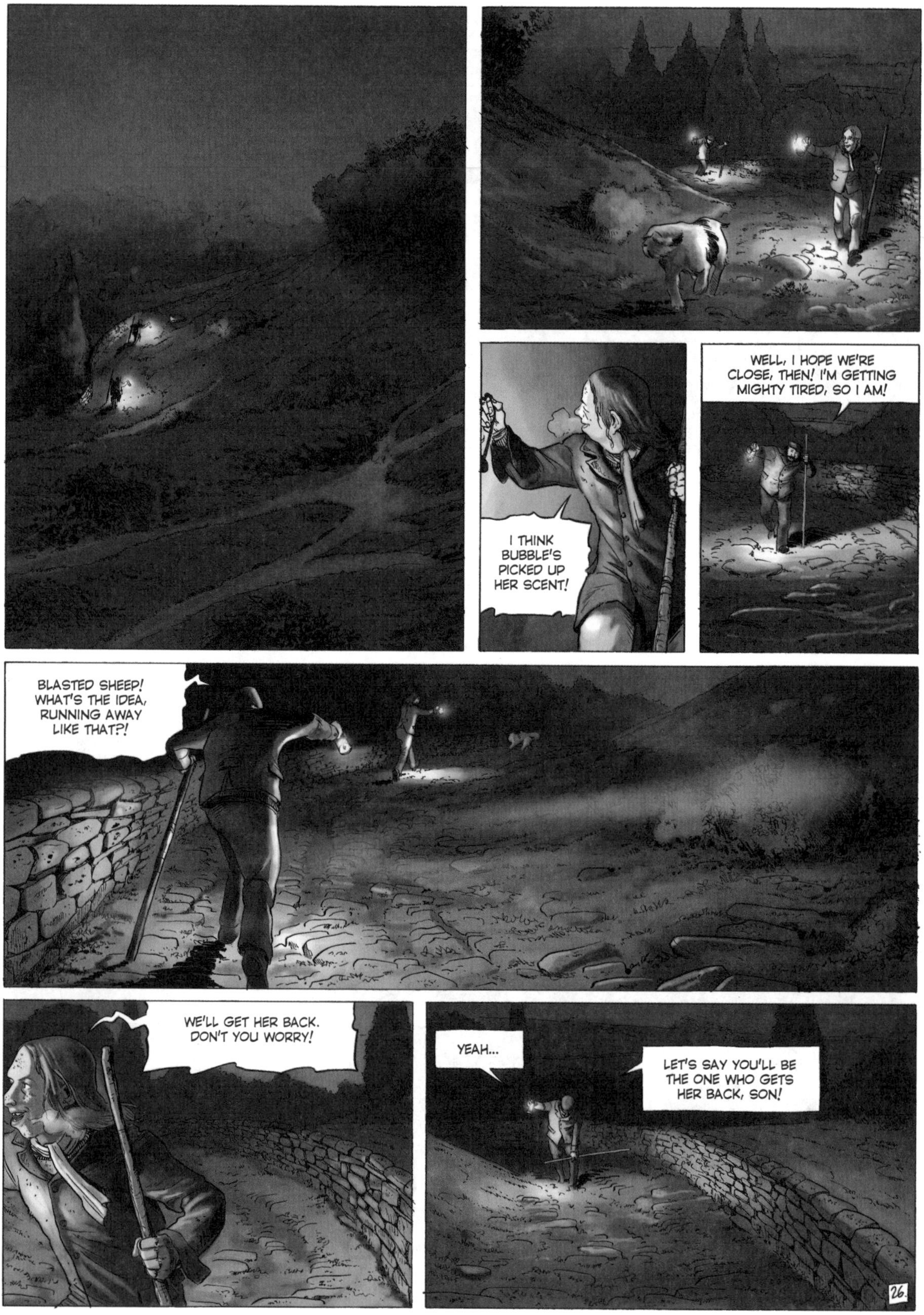
I THINK BUBBLE'S PICKED UP HER SCENT!
WELL, I HOPE WE'RE CLOSE, THEN! I'M GETTING MIGHTY TIRED, SO I AM!
BLASTED SHEEP! WHAT'S THE IDEA, RUNNING AWAY LIKE THAT?!
WE'LL GET HER BACK. DON'T YOU WORRY!
YEAH...
LET'S SAY YOU'LL BE THE ONE WHO GETS HER BACK, SON!
26.

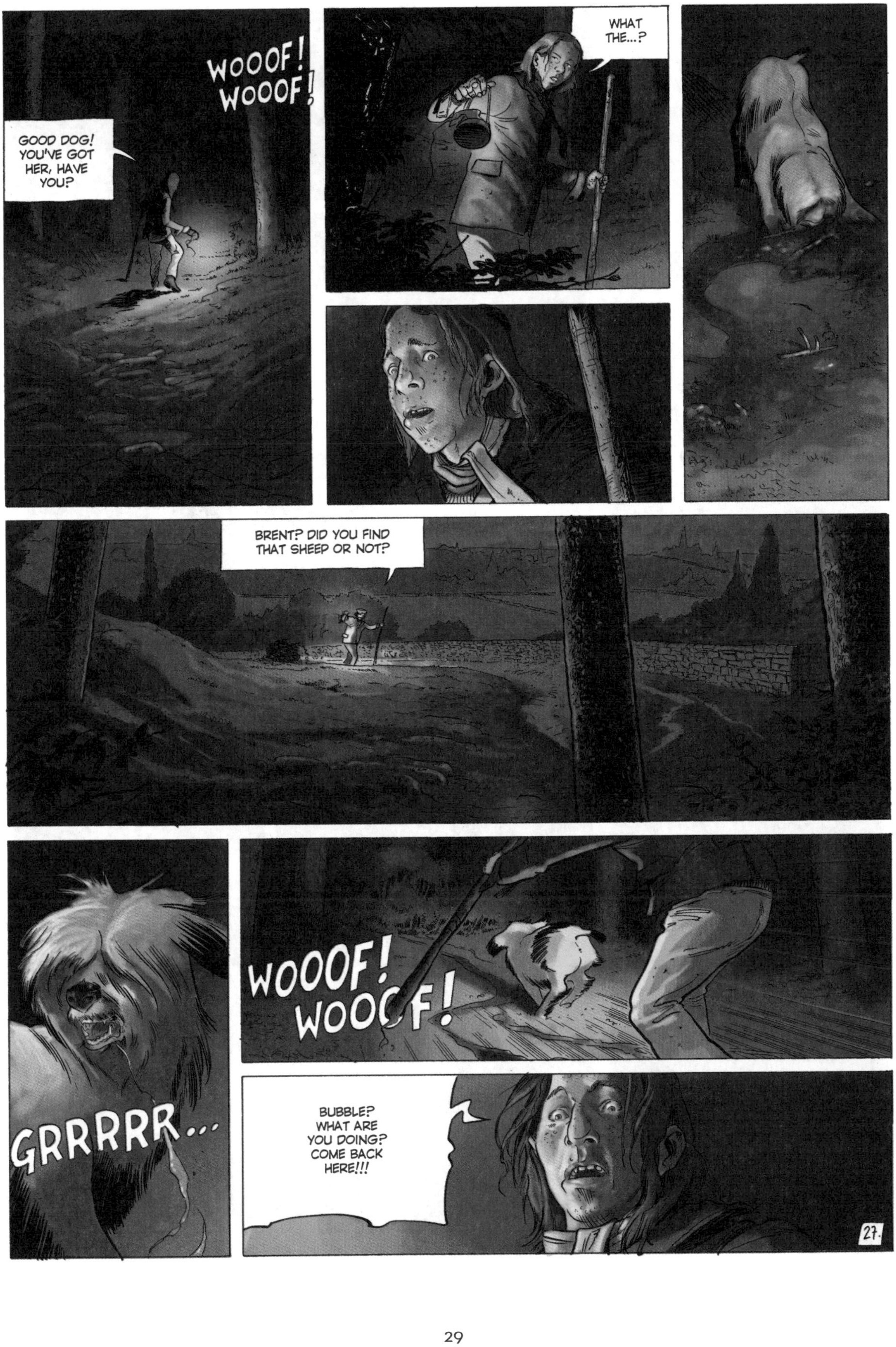
WOOOF! WOOOF!
GOOD DOG! YOU'VE GOT HER, HAVE YOU?
WHAT THE...?
BRENT? DID YOU FIND THAT SHEEP OR NOT?
GRRRRR...
WOOOF! WOOOF!
BUBBLE? WHAT ARE YOU DOING? COME BACK HERE!!!
27.

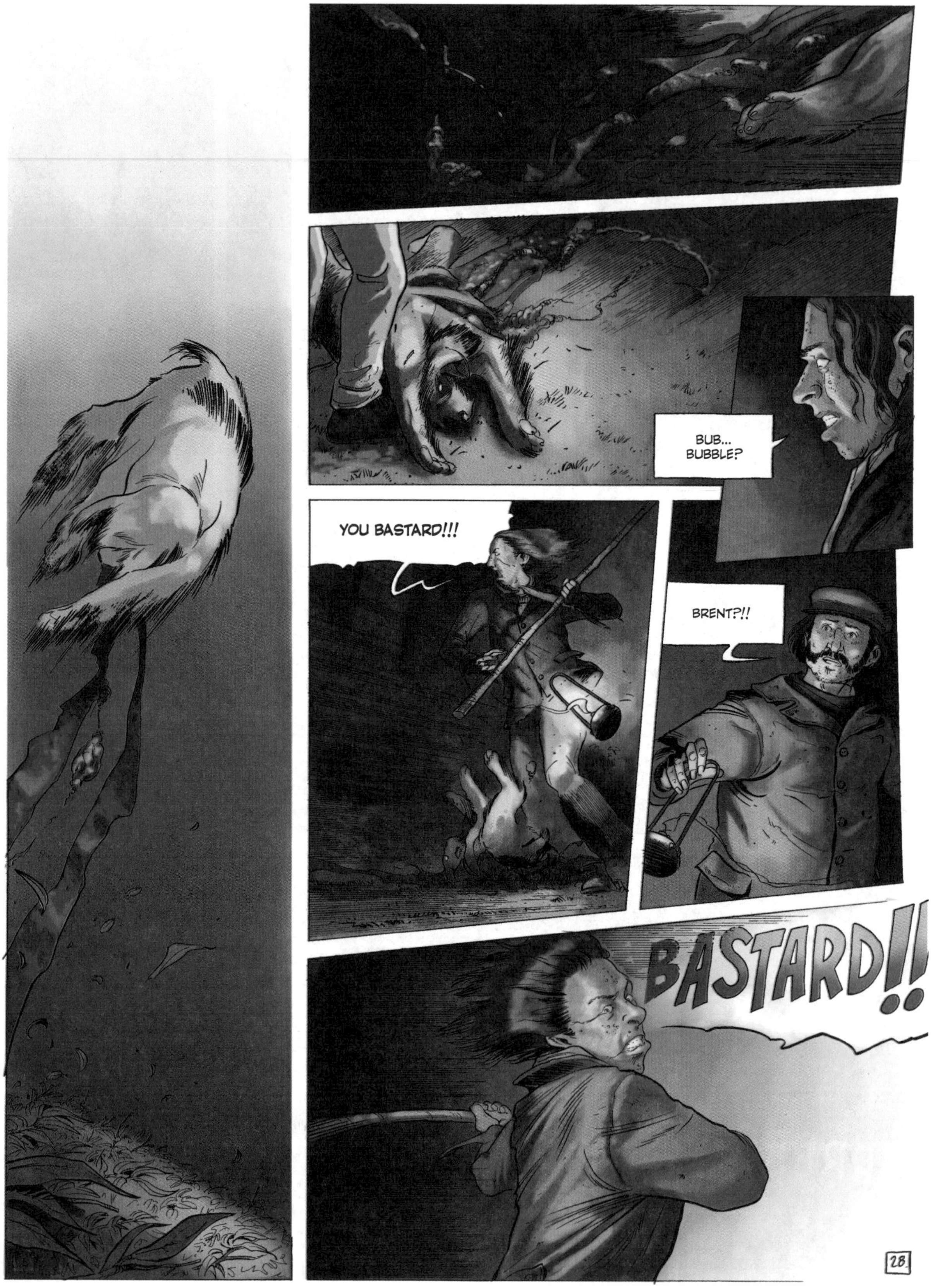
BUB...
BUBBLE?
YOU BASTARD!!!
BRENT?!!
BASTARD!!
28

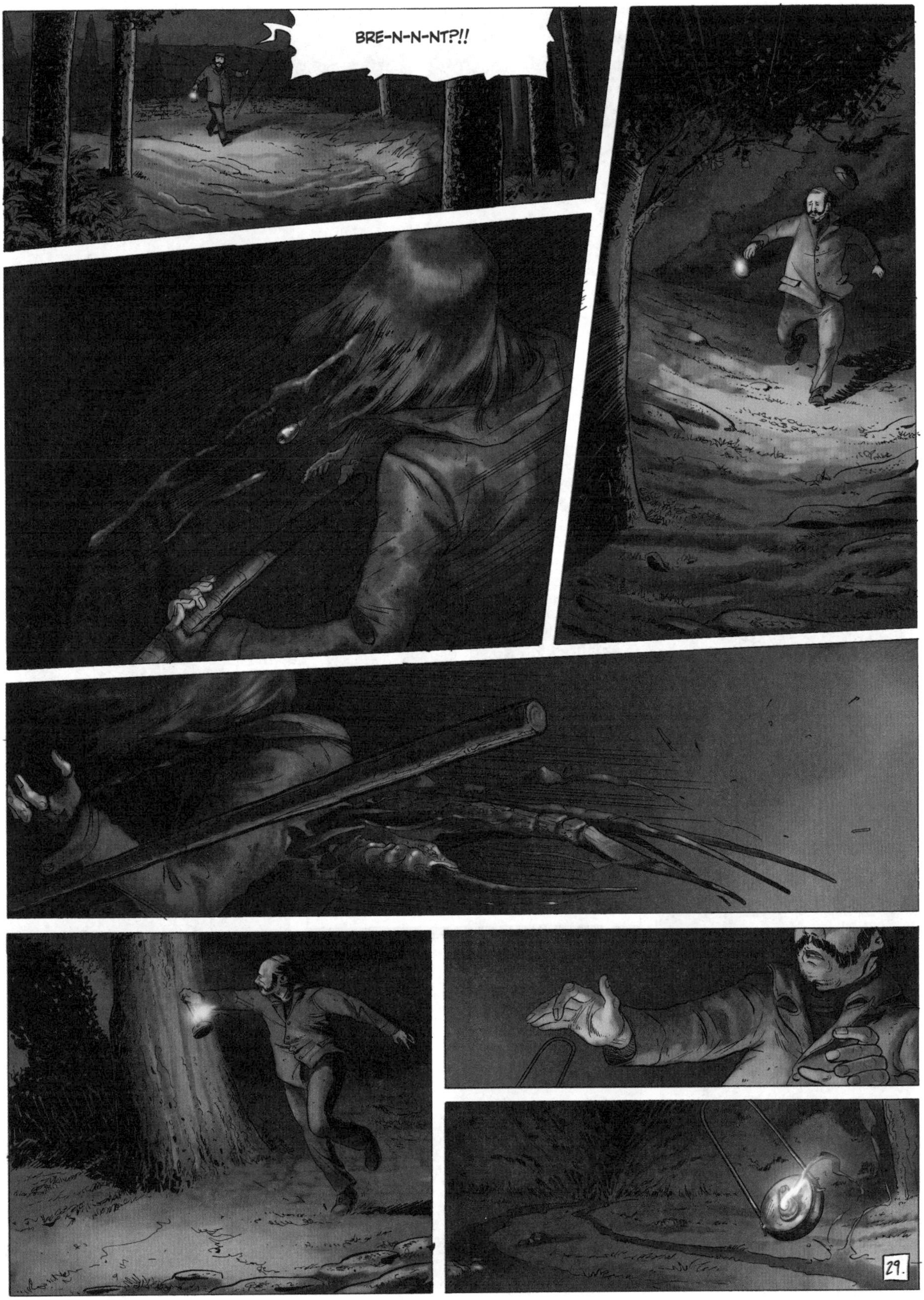
BRE-N-N-NT?!!
29.

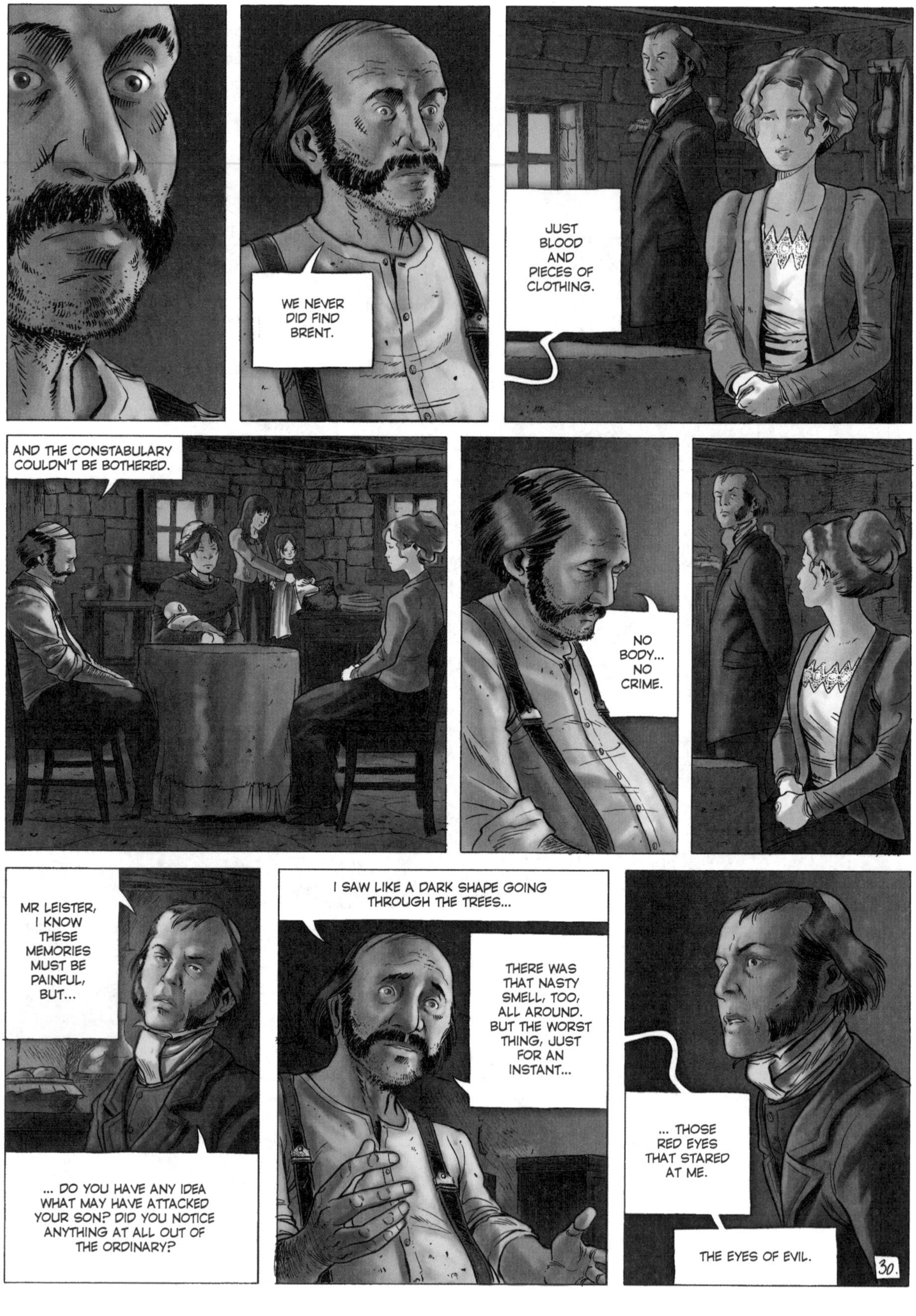
WE NEVER DID FIND BRENT.
JUST BLOOD AND PIECES OF CLOTHING.
AND THE CONSTABULARY COULDN'T BE BOTHERED.
NO BODY... NO CRIME.
MR LEISTER, I KNOW THESE MEMORIES MUST BE PAINFUL, BUT...
... DO YOU HAVE ANY IDEA WHAT MAY HAVE ATTACKED YOUR SON? DID YOU NOTICE ANYTHING AT ALL OUT OF THE ORDINARY?
I SAW LIKE A DARK SHAPE GOING THROUGH THE TREES...
THERE WAS THAT NASTY SMELL, TOO, ALL AROUND. BUT THE WORST THING, JUST FOR AN INSTANT...
... THOSE RED EYES THAT STARED AT ME.
THE EYES OF EVIL.
30.

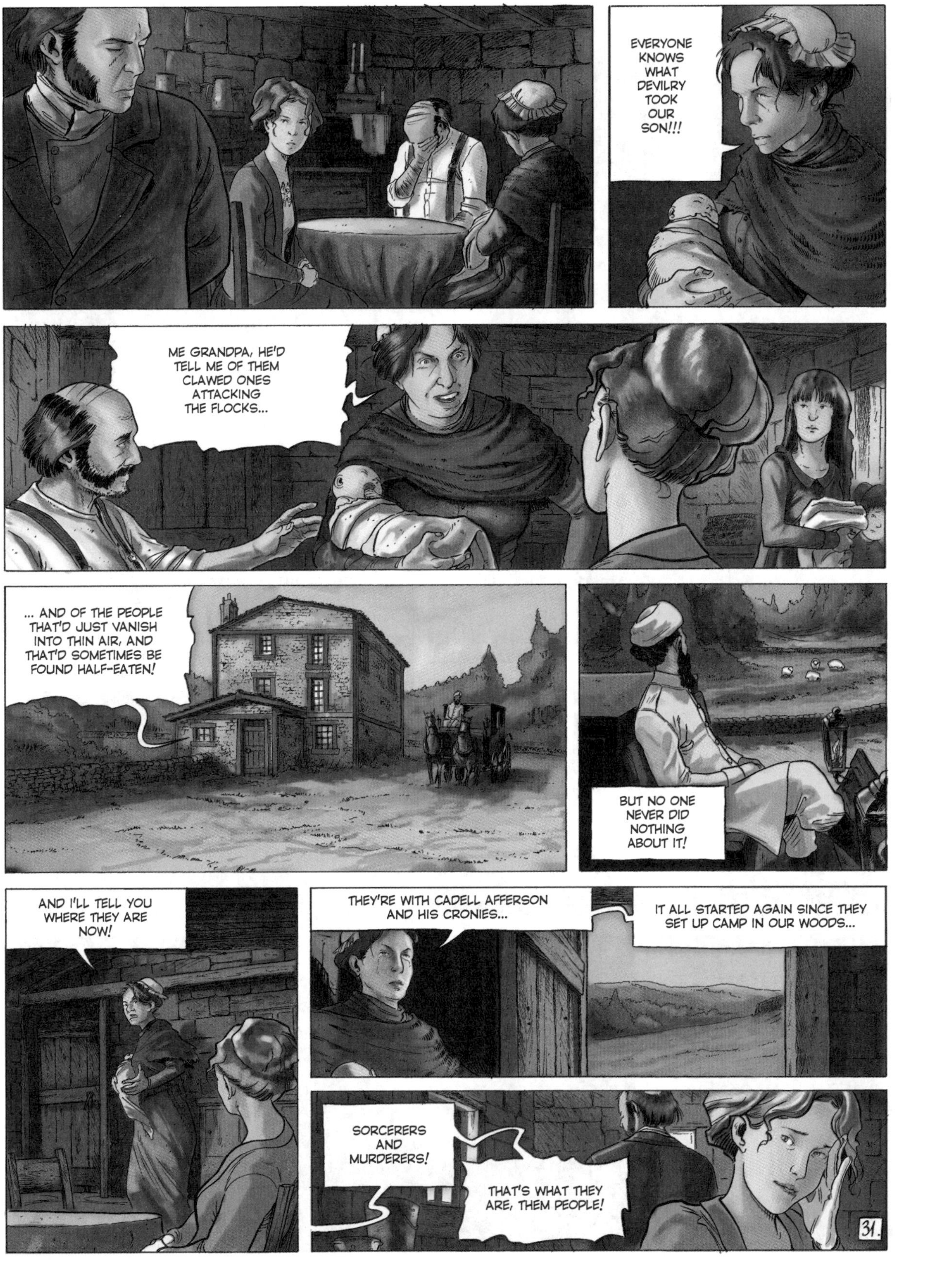
EVERYONE KNOWS WHAT DEVILRY TOOK OUR SON!!!
ME GRANDPA, HE'D TELL ME OF THEM CLAWED ONES ATTACKING THE FLOCKS...
... AND OF THE PEOPLE THAT'D JUST VANISH INTO THIN AIR, AND THAT'D SOMETIMES BE FOUND HALF-EATEN!
BUT NO ONE NEVER DID NOTHING ABOUT IT!
AND I'LL TELL YOU WHERE THEY ARE NOW!
THEY'RE WITH CADELL AFFERSON AND HIS CRONIES...
IT ALL STARTED AGAIN SINCE THEY SET UP CAMP IN OUR WOODS...
SORCERERS AND MURDERERS!
THAT'S WHAT THEY ARE, THEM PEOPLE!
31.

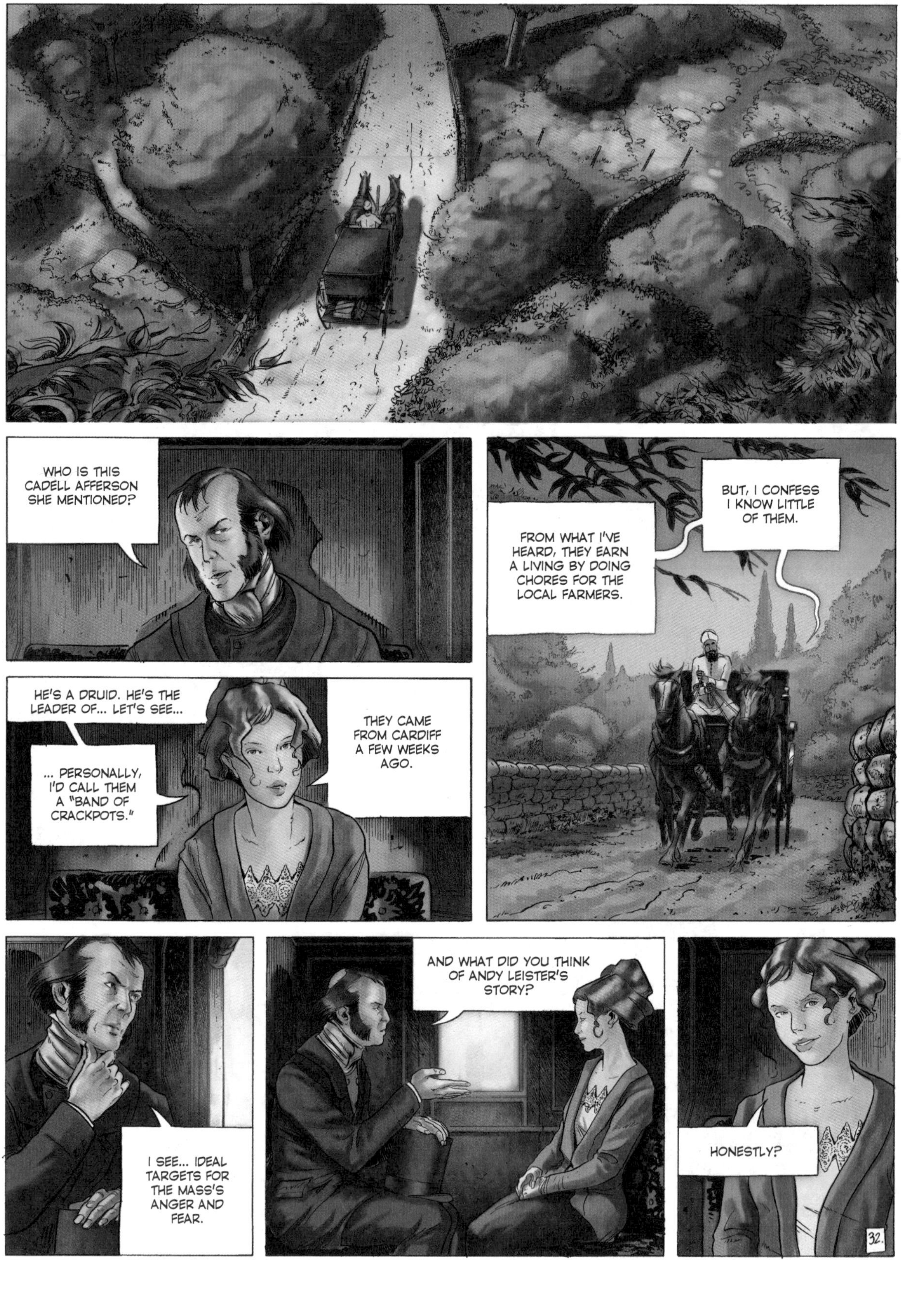
WHO IS THIS CADELL AFFERSON SHE MENTIONED?
FROM WHAT I'VE HEARD, THEY EARN A LIVING BY DOING CHORES FOR THE LOCAL FARMERS.
BUT, I CONFESS I KNOW LITTLE OF THEM.
HE'S A DRUID. HE'S THE LEADER OF... LET'S SEE...
... PERSONALLY, I'D CALL THEM A "BAND OF CRACKPOTS."
THEY CAME FROM CARDIFF A FEW WEEKS AGO.
I SEE... IDEAL TARGETS FOR THE MASS'S ANGER AND FEAR.
AND WHAT DID YOU THINK OF ANDY LEISTER'S STORY?
HONESTLY?
32.

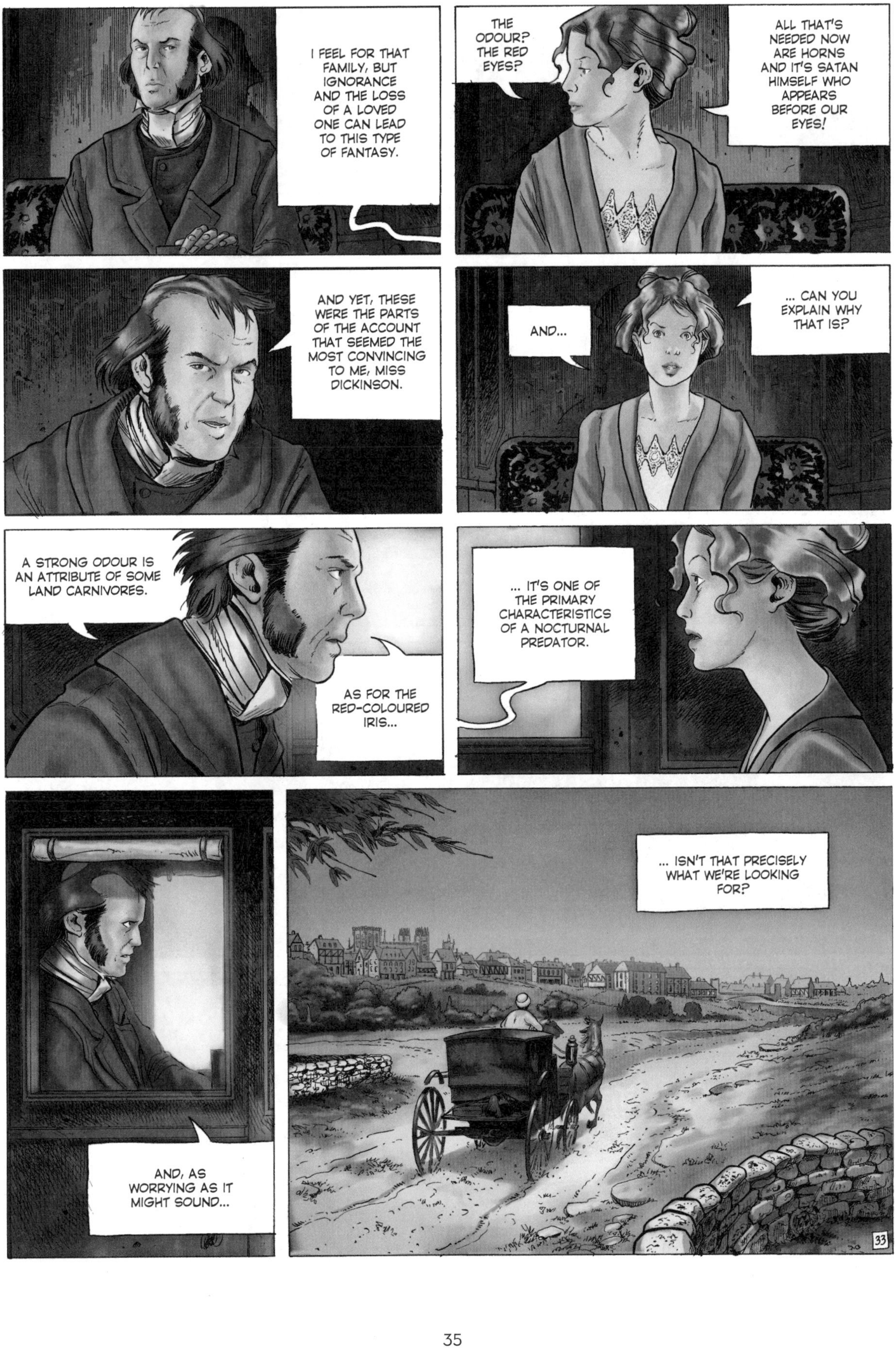
I FEEL FOR THAT FAMILY, BUT IGNORANCE AND THE LOSS OF A LOVED ONE CAN LEAD TO THIS TYPE OF FANTASY.
THE ODOUR? THE RED EYES?
ALL THAT'S NEEDED NOW ARE HORNS AND IT'S SATAN HIMSELF WHO APPEARS BEFORE OUR EYES!
AND YET, THESE WERE THE PARTS OF THE ACCOUNT THAT SEEMED THE MOST CONVINCING TO ME, MISS DICKINSON.
AND...
... CAN YOU EXPLAIN WHY THAT IS?
A STRONG ODOUR IS AN ATTRIBUTE OF SOME LAND CARNIVORES.
AS FOR THE RED-COLOURED IRIS...
... IT'S ONE OF THE PRIMARY CHARACTERISTICS OF A NOCTURNAL PREDATOR.
AND, AS WORRYING AS IT MIGHT SOUND...
... ISN'T THAT PRECISELY WHAT WE'RE LOOKING FOR?
33

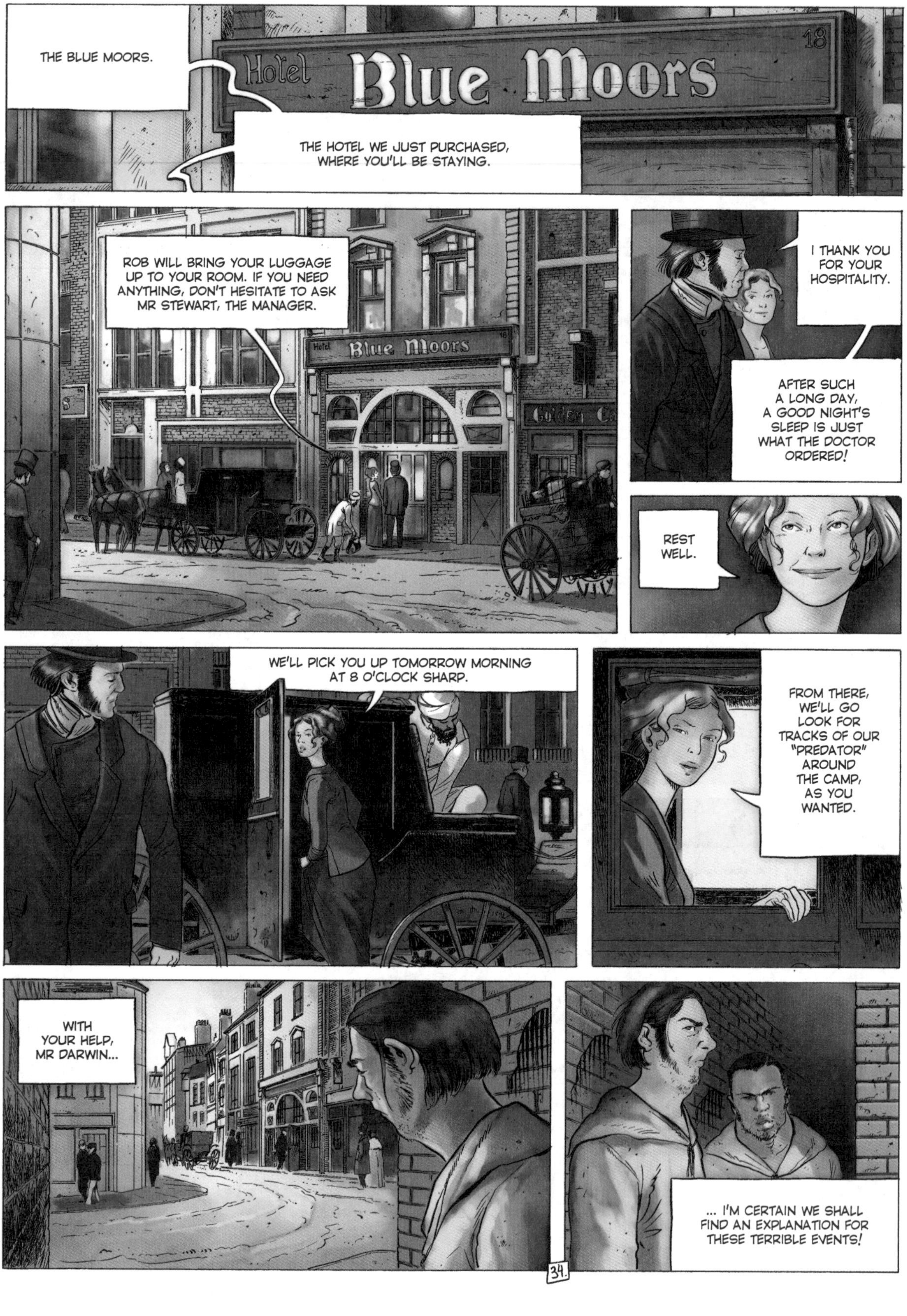
THE BLUE MOORS.
Hotel Blue Moors 18
THE HOTEL WE JUST PURCHASED, WHERE YOU'LL BE STAYING.
ROB WILL BRING YOUR LUGGAGE UP TO YOUR ROOM. IF YOU NEED ANYTHING, DON'T HESITATE TO ASK MR STEWART, THE MANAGER.
Hotel Blue Moors
I THANK YOU FOR YOUR HOSPITALITY.
AFTER SUCH A LONG DAY, A GOOD NIGHT'S SLEEP IS JUST WHAT THE DOCTOR ORDERED!
REST WELL.
WE'LL PICK YOU UP TOMORROW MORNING AT 8 O'CLOCK SHARP.
FROM THERE, WE'LL GO LOOK FOR TRACKS OF OUR "PREDATOR" AROUND THE CAMP, AS YOU WANTED.
WITH YOUR HELP, MR DARWIN...
... I'M CERTAIN WE SHALL FIND AN EXPLANATION FOR THESE TERRIBLE EVENTS!
34.

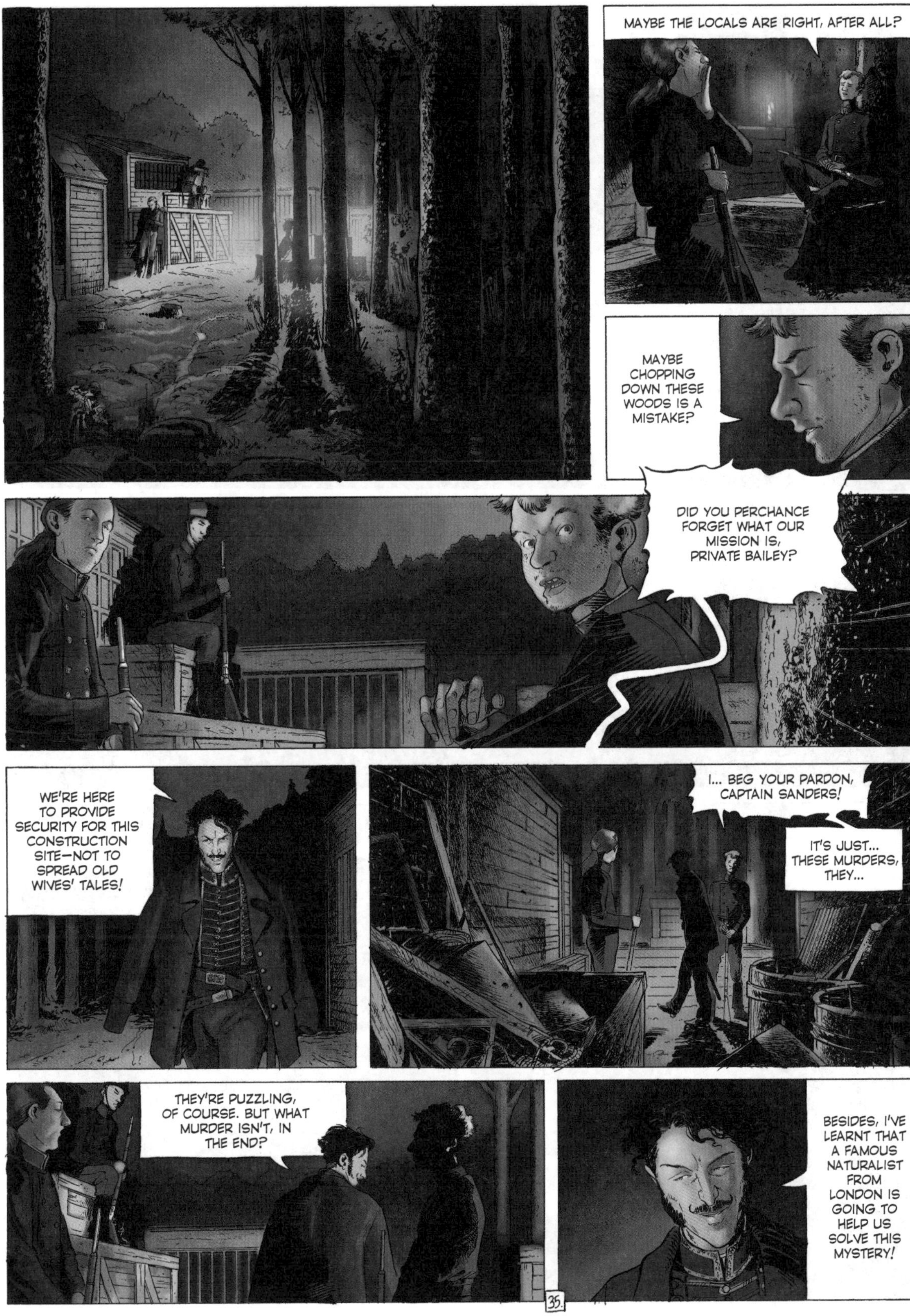
MAYBE THE LOCALS ARE RIGHT, AFTER ALL?
MAYBE CHOPPING DOWN THESE WOODS IS A MISTAKE?
DID YOU PERCHANCE FORGET WHAT OUR MISSION IS, PRIVATE BAILEY?
WE'RE HERE TO PROVIDE SECURITY FOR THIS CONSTRUCTION SITE—NOT TO SPREAD OLD WIVES' TALES!
I... BEG YOUR PARDON, CAPTAIN SANDERS!
IT'S JUST... THESE MURDERS, THEY...
THEY'RE PUZZLING, OF COURSE. BUT WHAT MURDER ISN'T, IN THE END?
BESIDES, I'VE LEARNT THAT A FAMOUS NATURALIST FROM LONDON IS GOING TO HELP US SOLVE THIS MYSTERY!
35.

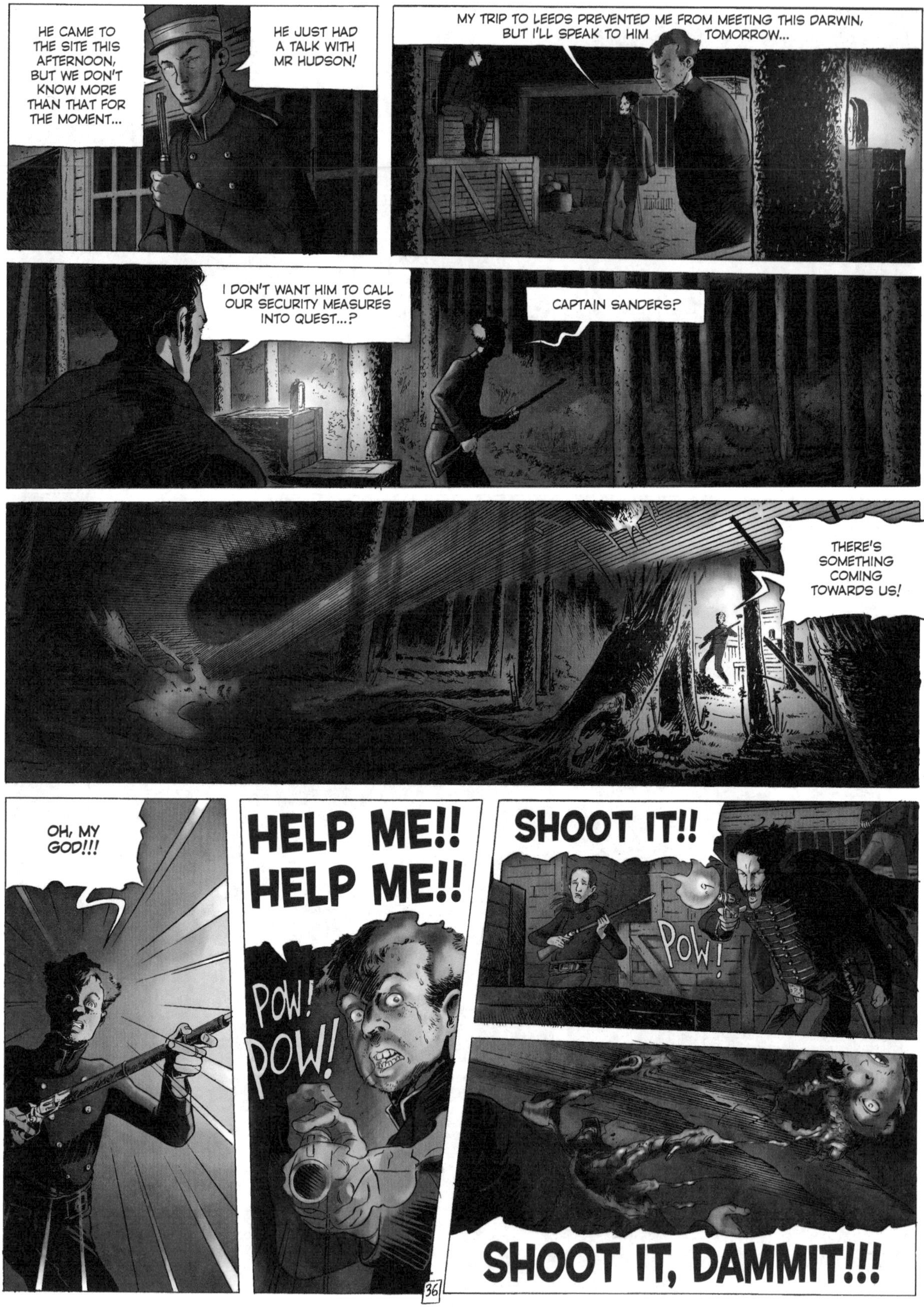
HE CAME TO THE SITE THIS AFTERNOON, BUT WE DON'T KNOW MORE THAN THAT FOR THE MOMENT...
HE JUST HAD A TALK WITH MR HUDSON!
MY TRIP TO LEEDS PREVENTED ME FROM MEETING THIS DARWIN, BUT I'LL SPEAK TO HIM TOMORROW...
I DON'T WANT HIM TO CALL OUR SECURITY MEASURES INTO QUEST...?
CAPTAIN SANDERS?
THERE'S SOMETHING COMING TOWARDS US!
OH, MY GOD!!!
HELP ME!! HELP ME!!
POW! POW!
SHOOT IT!!
POW!
SHOOT IT, DAMMIT!!!
36

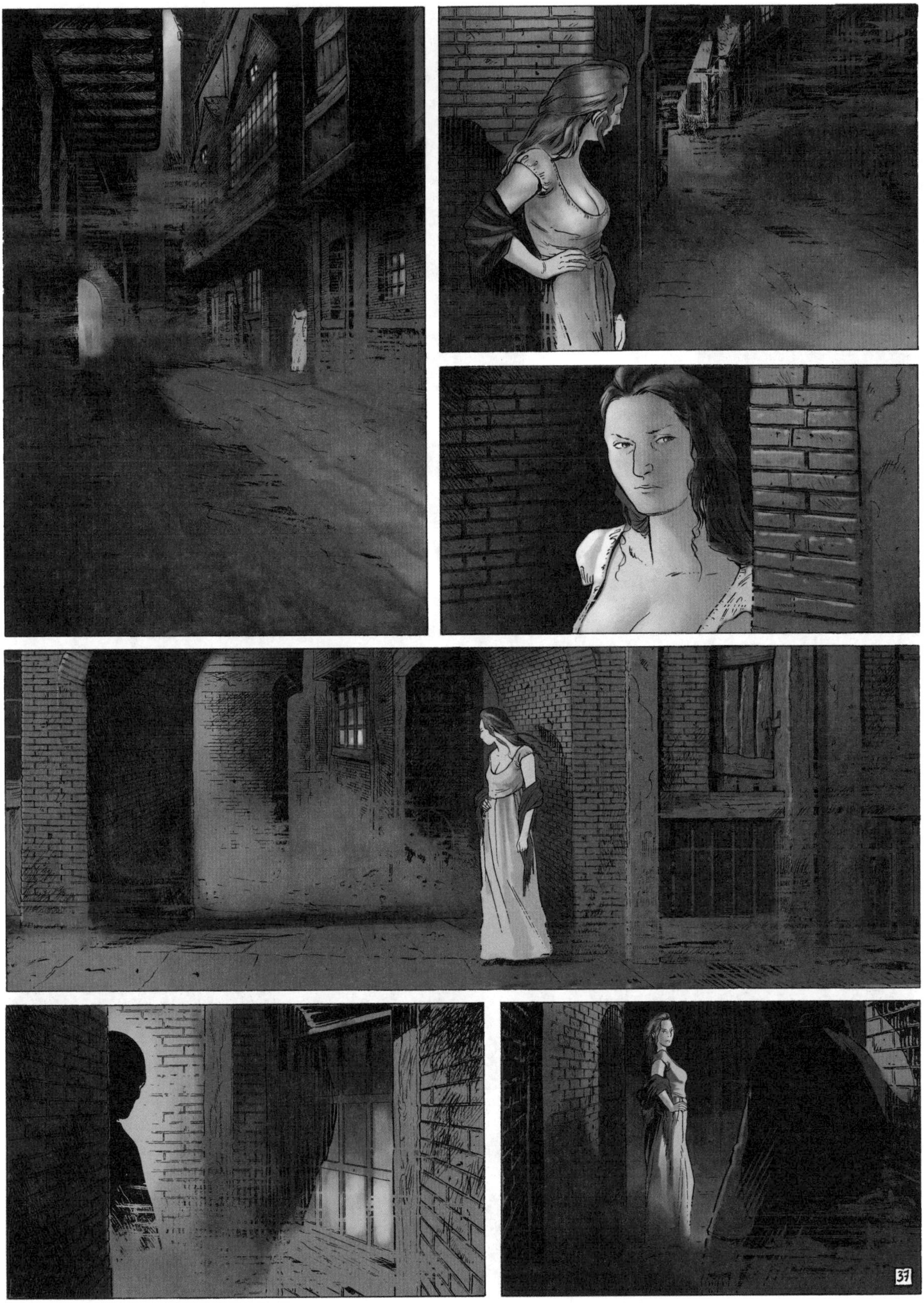
37

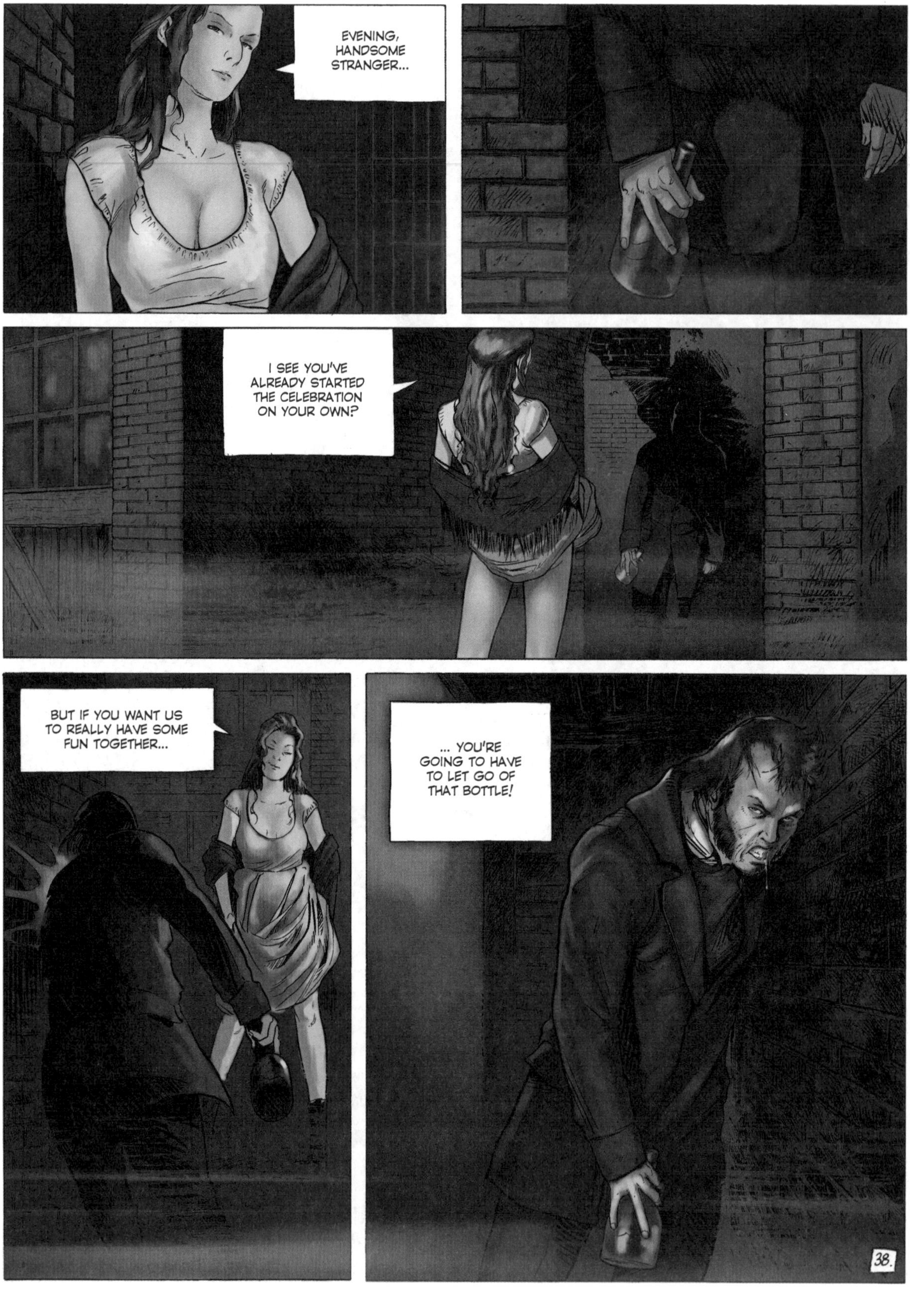
EVENING, HANDSOME STRANGER...
I SEE YOU'VE ALREADY STARTED THE CELEBRATION ON YOUR OWN?
BUT IF YOU WANT US TO REALLY HAVE SOME FUN TOGETHER...
... YOU'RE GOING TO HAVE TO LET GO OF THAT BOTTLE!
38.

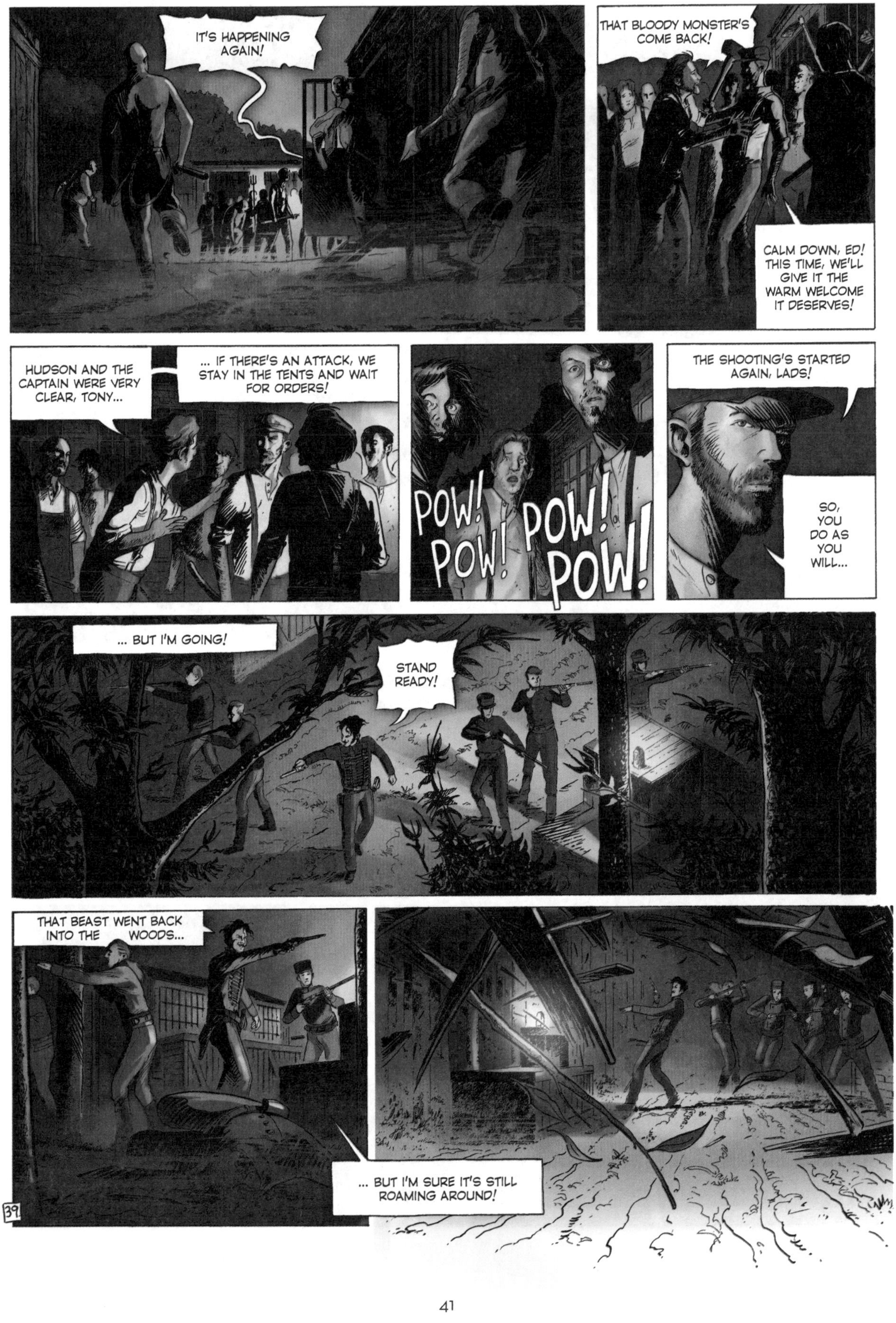

IT'S HAPPENING AGAIN!
THAT BLOODY MONSTER'S COME BACK!
CALM DOWN, ED! THIS TIME, WE'LL GIVE IT THE WARM WELCOME IT DESERVES!
HUDSON AND THE CAPTAIN WERE VERY CLEAR, TONY...
... IF THERE'S AN ATTACK, WE STAY IN THE TENTS AND WAIT FOR ORDERS!
POW! POW! POW! POW!
THE SHOOTING'S STARTED AGAIN, LADS!
SO, YOU DO AS YOU WILL...
... BUT I'M GOING!
STAND READY!
THAT BEAST WENT BACK INTO THE WOODS...
... BUT I'M SURE IT'S STILL ROAMING AROUND!
39

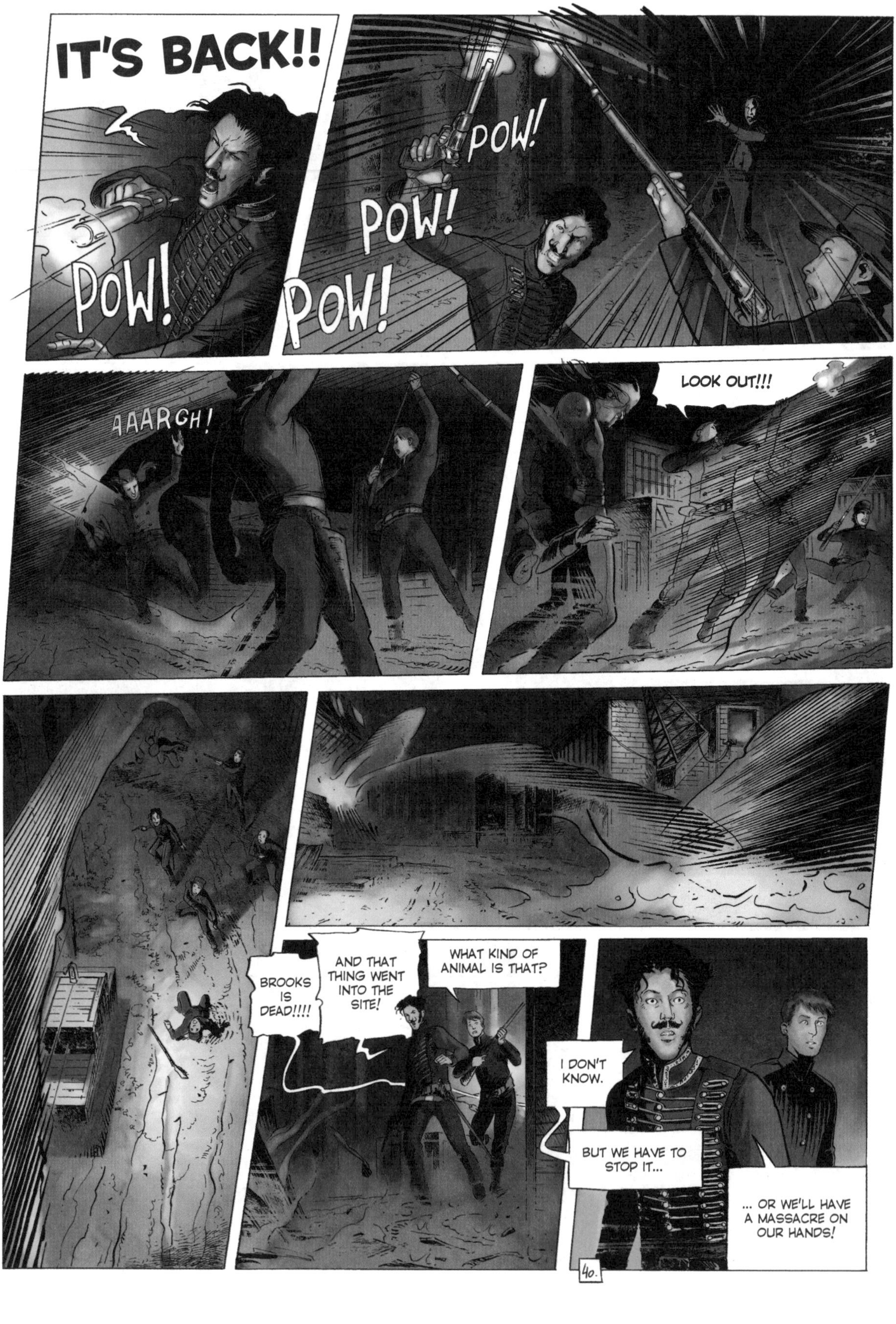
IT'S BACK!!
POW!
POW!
POW!
POW!
AAARGH!
LOOK OUT!!!
BROOKS IS DEAD!!!!
AND THAT THING WENT INTO THE SITE!
WHAT KIND OF ANIMAL IS THAT?
I DON'T KNOW.
BUT WE HAVE TO STOP IT...
... OR WE'LL HAVE A MASSACRE ON OUR HANDS!
40.

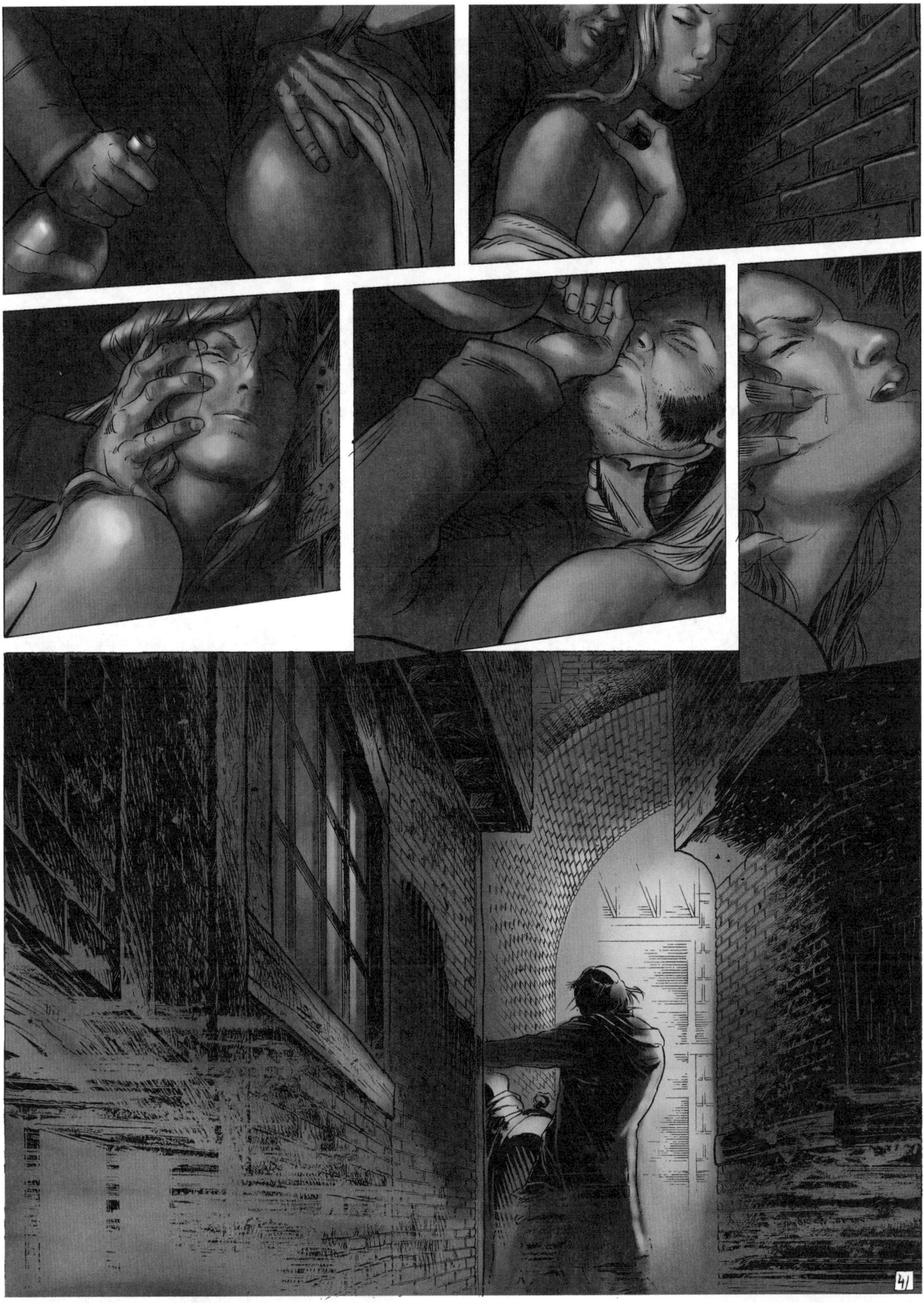
41

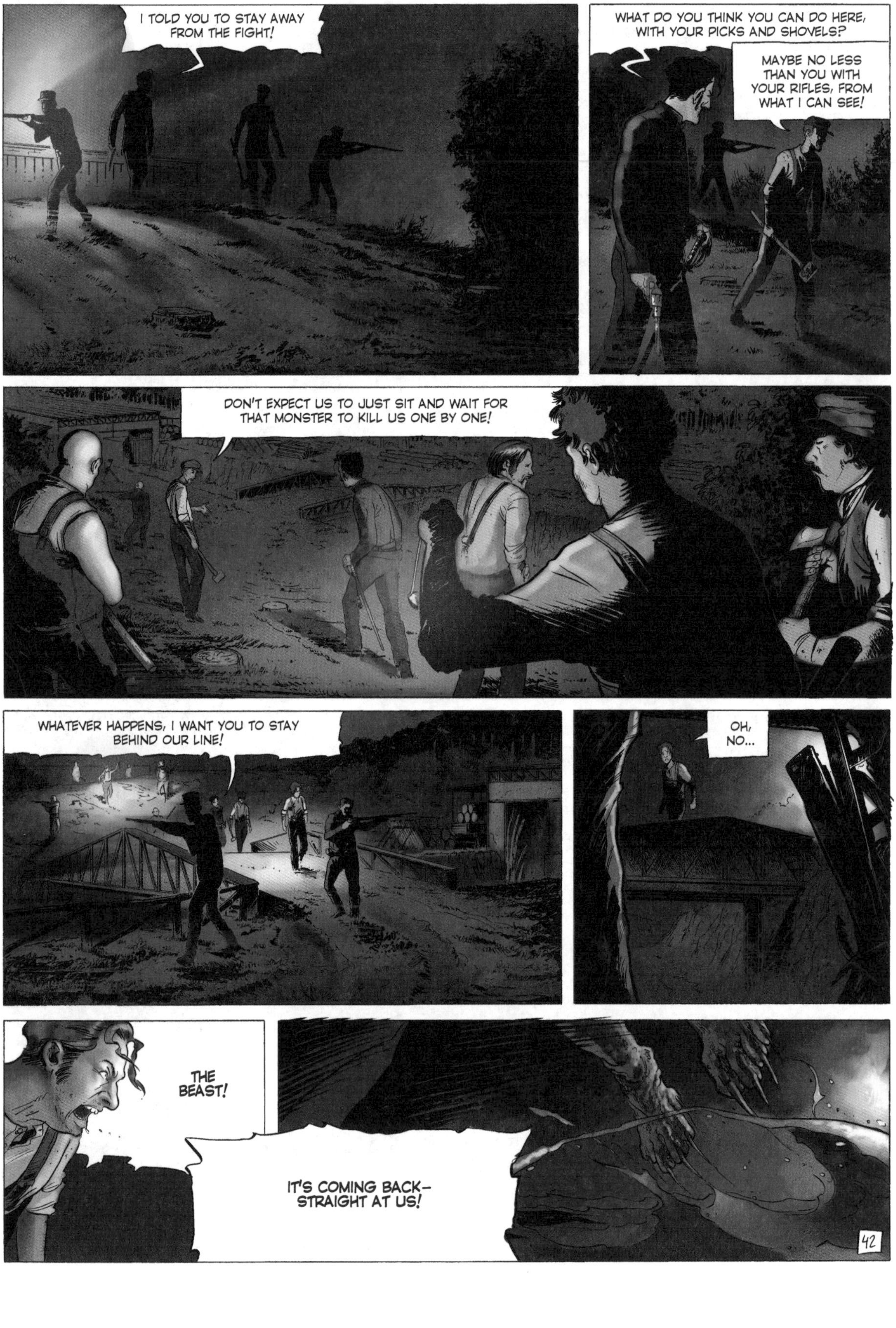
I TOLD YOU TO STAY AWAY FROM THE FIGHT!
WHAT DO YOU THINK YOU CAN DO HERE, WITH YOUR PICKS AND SHOVELS?
MAYBE NO LESS THAN YOU WITH YOUR RIFLES, FROM WHAT I CAN SEE!
DON'T EXPECT US TO JUST SIT AND WAIT FOR THAT MONSTER TO KILL US ONE BY ONE!
WHATEVER HAPPENS, I WANT YOU TO STAY BEHIND OUR LINE!
OH, NO...
THE BEAST!
IT'S COMING BACK-STRAIGHT AT US!
42

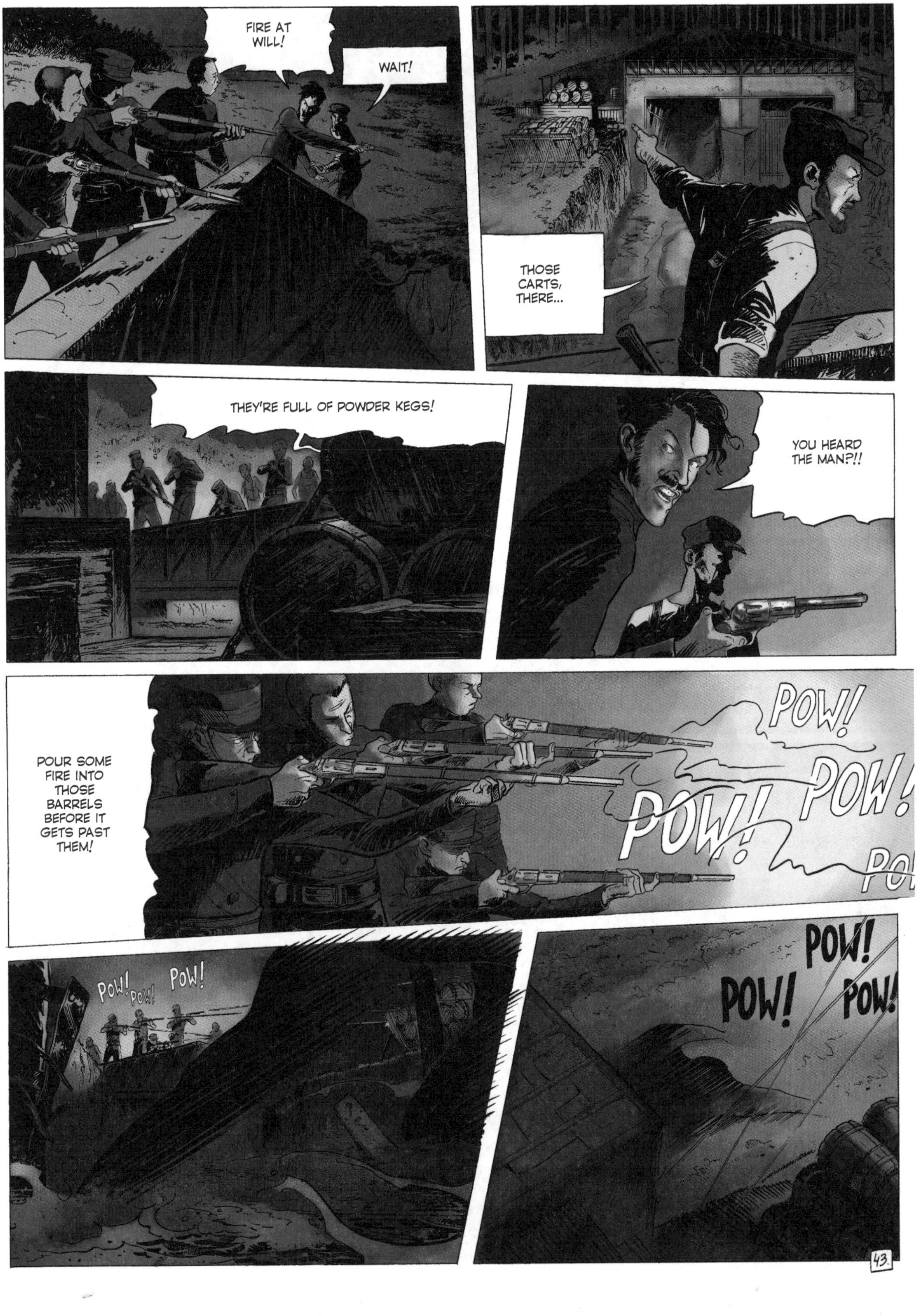
FIRE AT WILL!
WAIT!
THOSE CARTS, THERE...
THEY'RE FULL OF POWDER KEGS!
YOU HEARD THE MAN?!!
POUR SOME FIRE INTO THOSE BARRELS BEFORE IT GETS PAST THEM!
POW!
POW!
POW!
POW!
POW!
POW!
POW!
POW!
POW!
POW!
43.

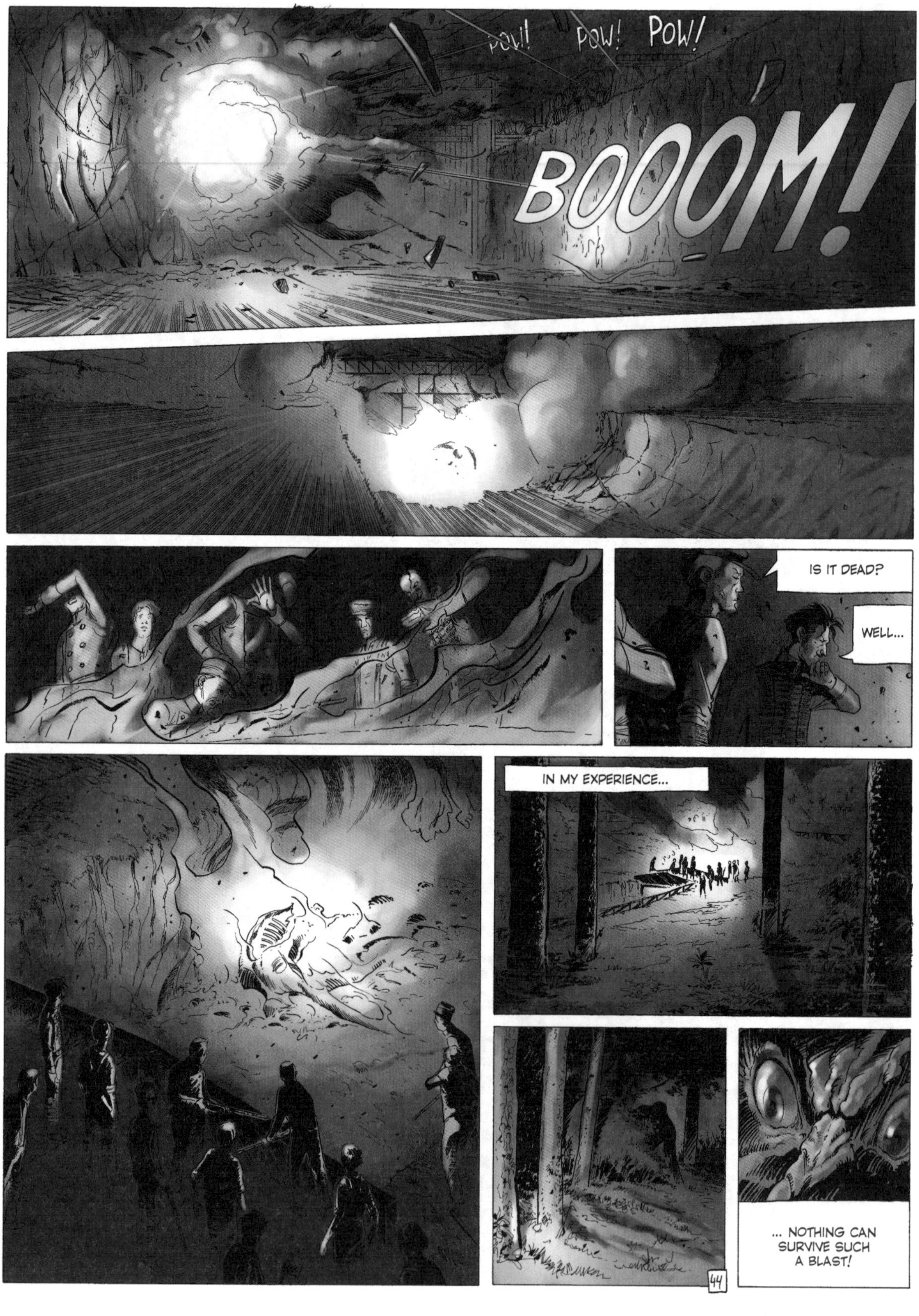
POW!
POW!
POW!
BOOOM!
IS IT DEAD?
WELL...
IN MY EXPERIENCE...
44
... NOTHING CAN SURVIVE SUCH A BLAST!

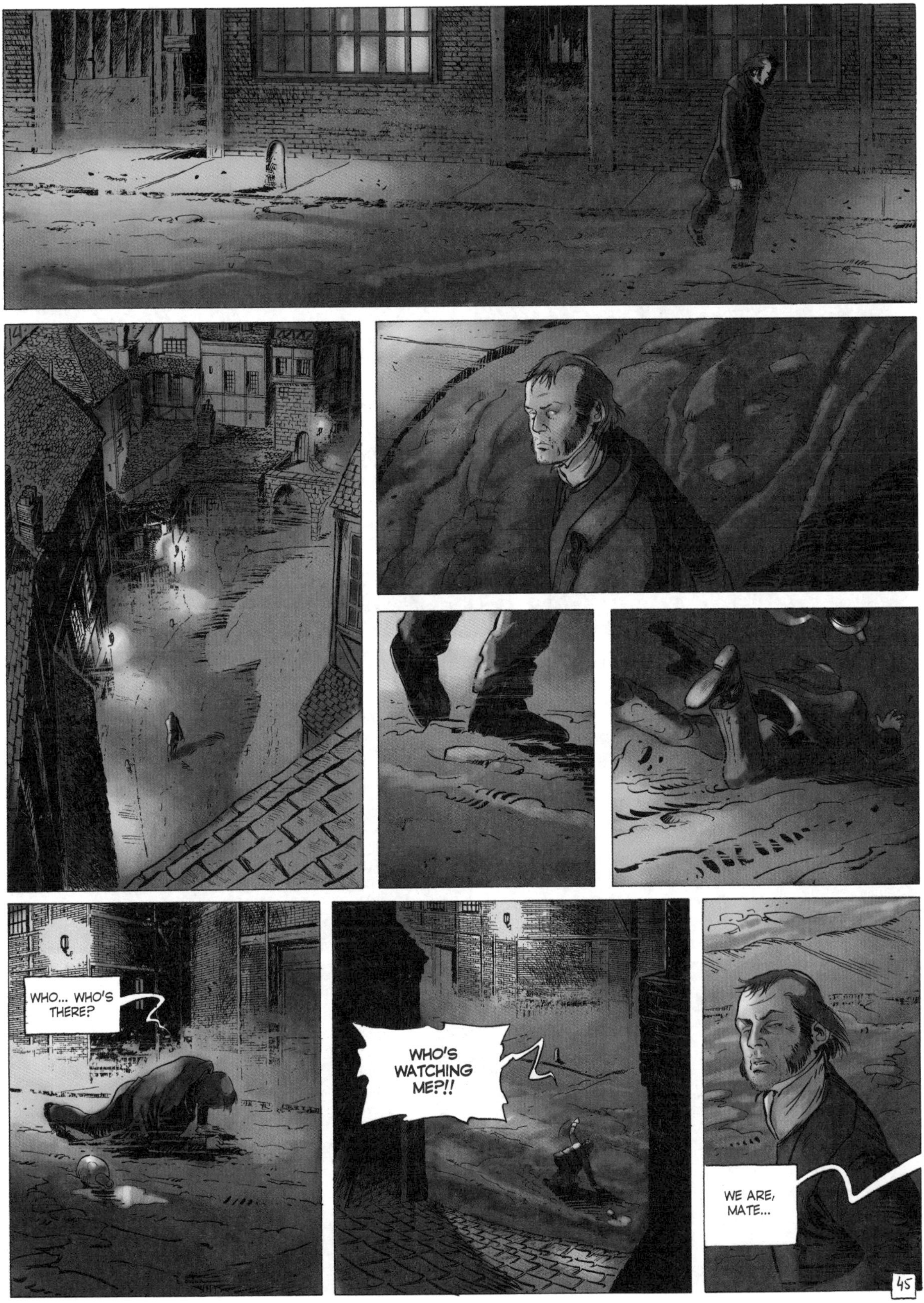
WHO... WHO'S THERE?
WHO'S WATCHING ME?!!
WE ARE, MATE...
45

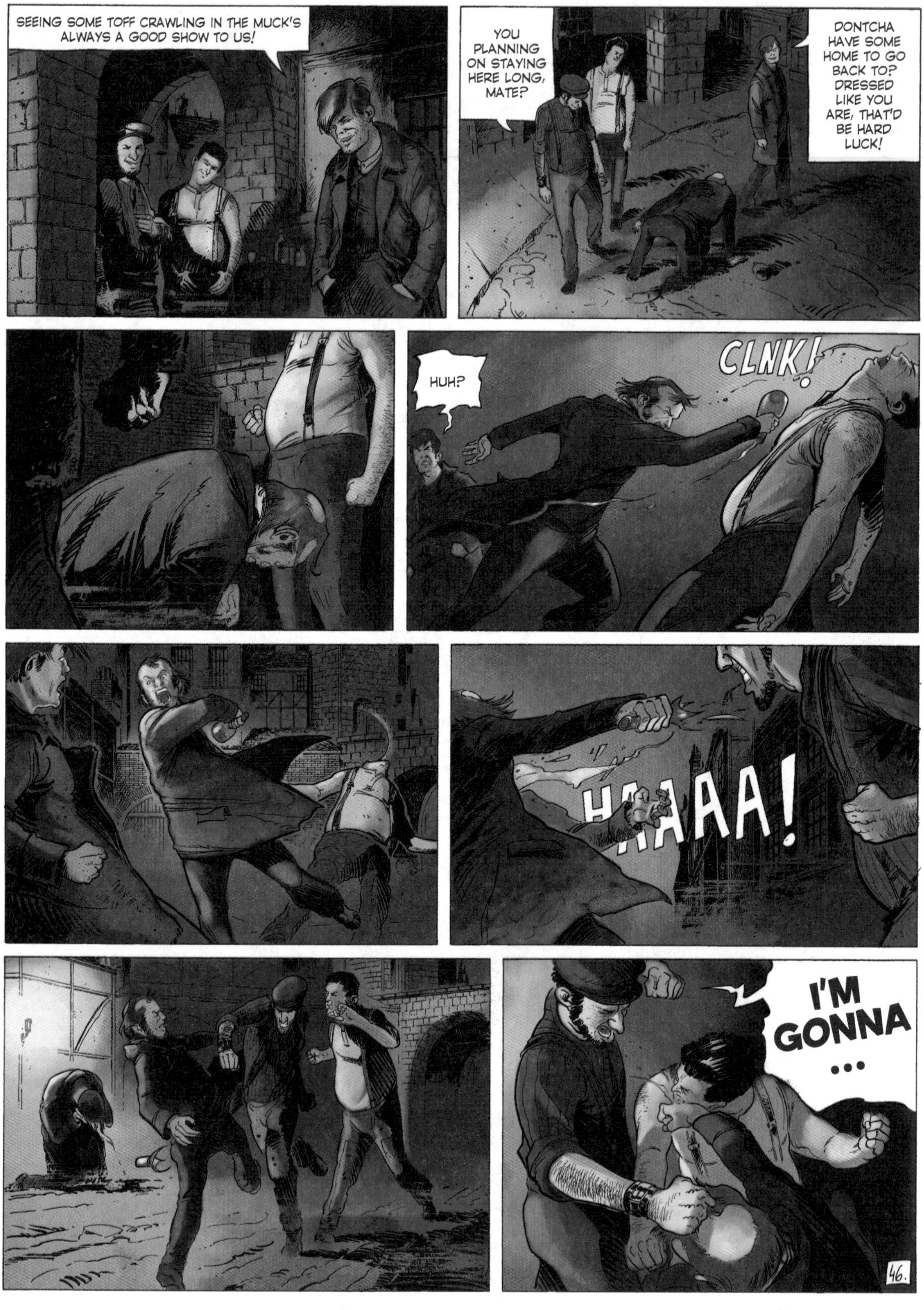
SEEING SOME TOFF CRAWLING IN THE MUCK'S ALWAYS A GOOD SHOW TO US!
YOU PLANNING ON STAYING HERE LONG, MATE?
DONTCHA HAVE SOME HOME TO GO BACK TO? DRESSED LIKE YOU ARE, THAT'D BE HARD LUCK!
HUH?
CLNK!
HAAAA!
I'M GONNA ...
46.

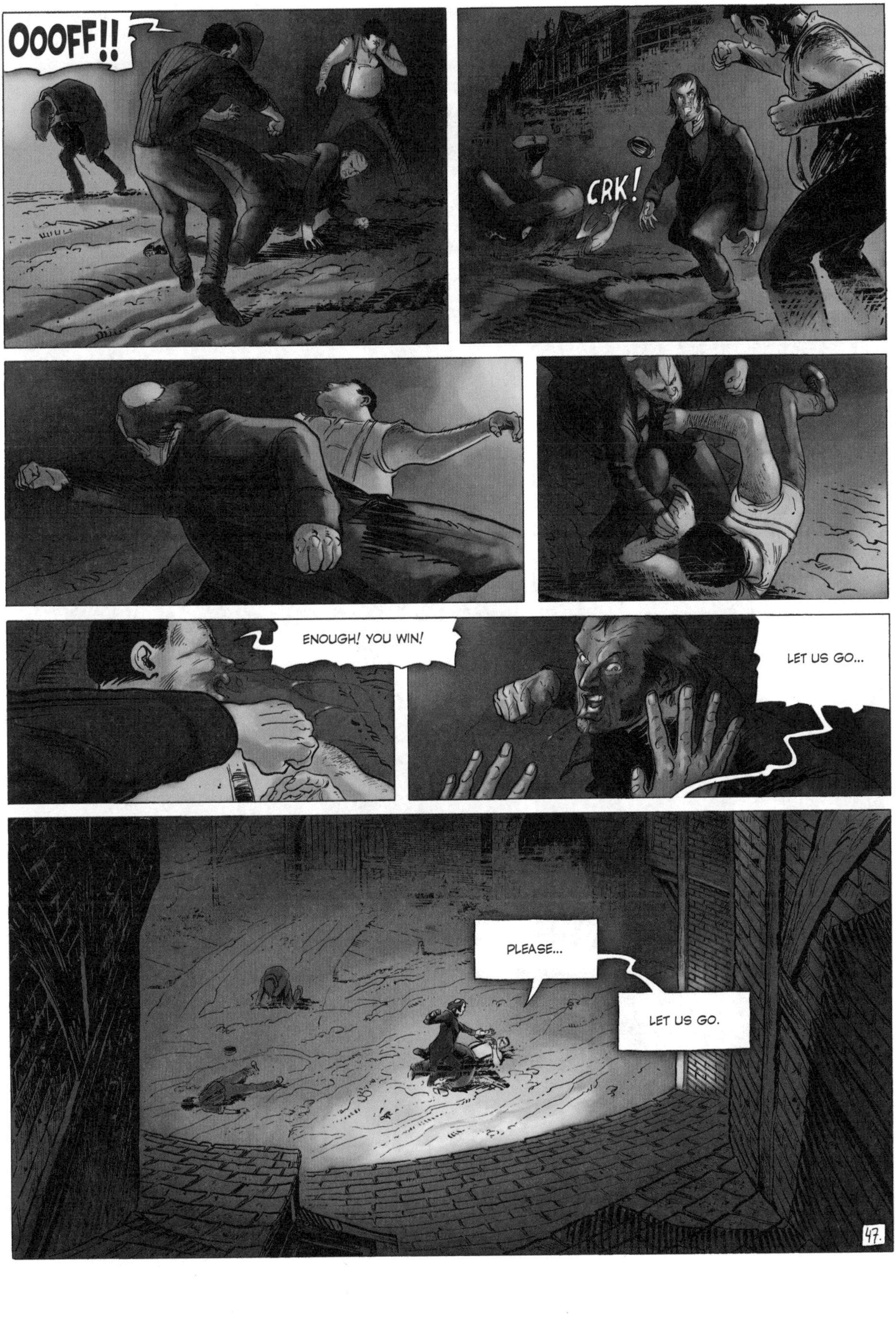
OOOFF!!
CRK!
ENOUGH! YOU WIN!
LET US GO...
PLEASE...
LET US GO.
47.

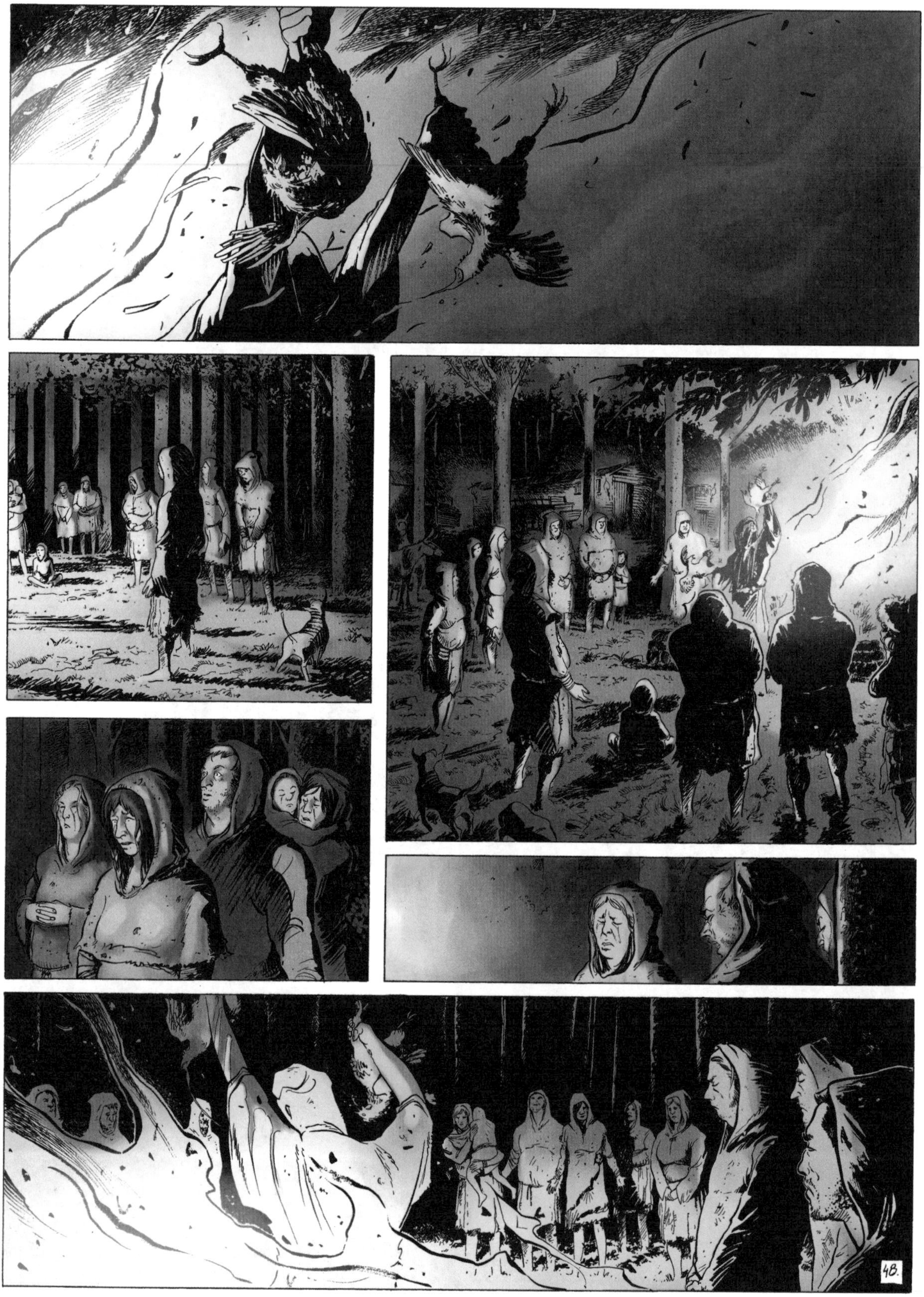
48.

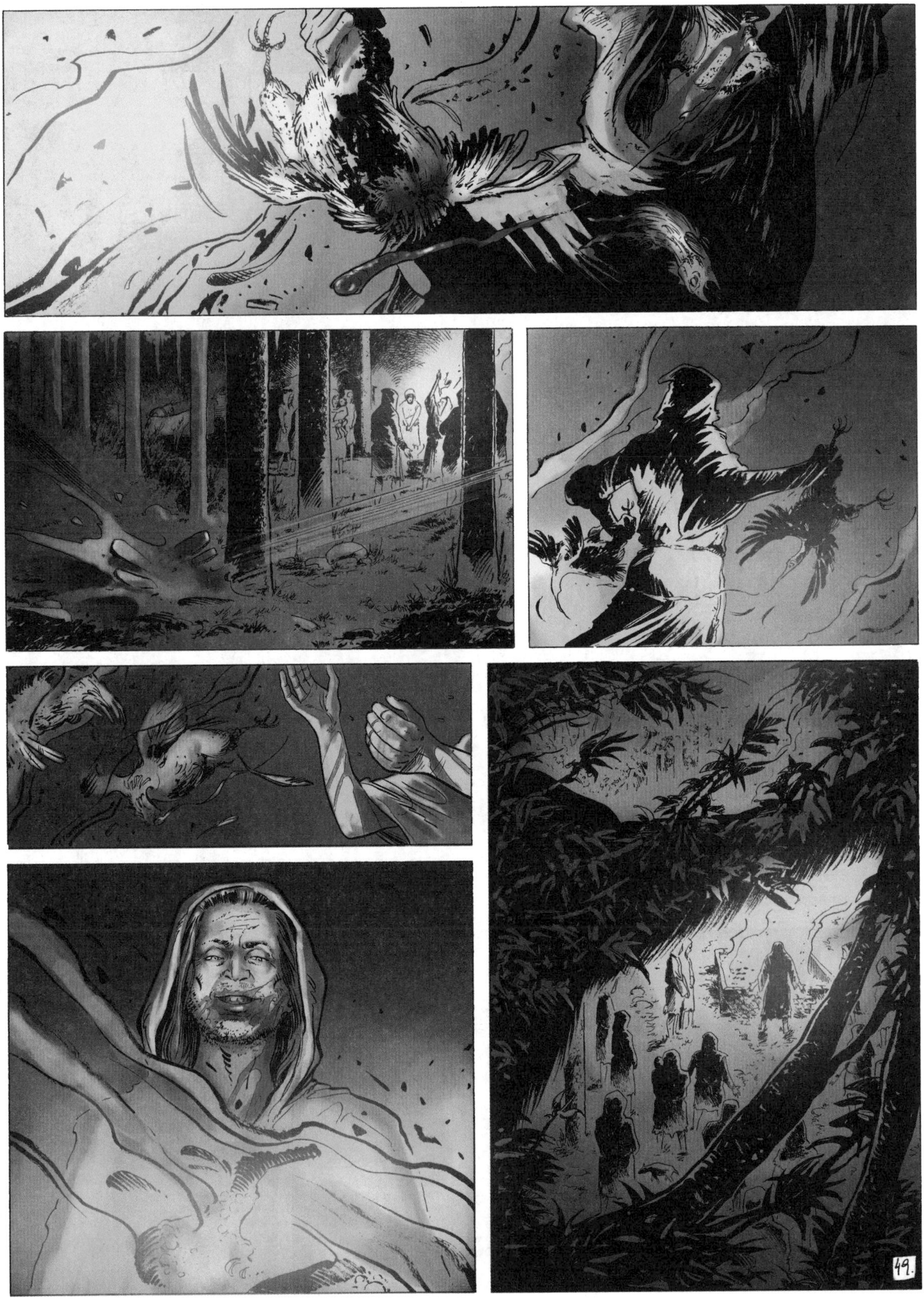
49.

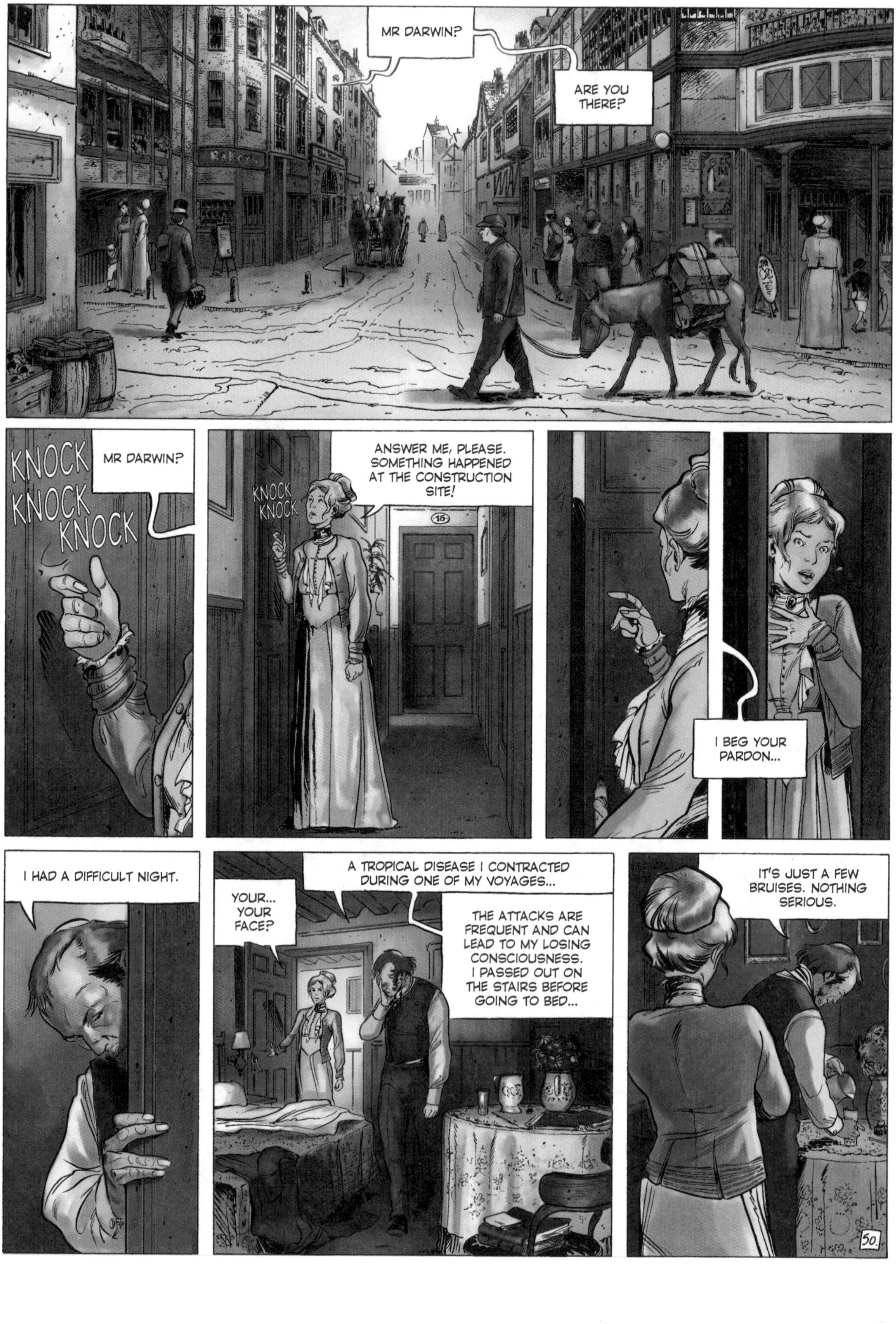

MR DARWIN?
ARE YOU THERE?
KNOCK KNOCK KNOCK
MR DARWIN?
KNOCK KNOCK
ANSWER ME, PLEASE. SOMETHING HAPPENED AT THE CONSTRUCTION SITE!
I BEG YOUR PARDON...
I HAD A DIFFICULT NIGHT.
YOUR... YOUR FACE?
A TROPICAL DISEASE I CONTRACTED DURING ONE OF MY VOYAGES...
THE ATTACKS ARE FREQUENT AND CAN LEAD TO MY LOSING CONSCIOUSNESS. I PASSED OUT ON THE STAIRS BEFORE GOING TO BED...
IT'S JUST A FEW BRUISES. NOTHING SERIOUS.
50.

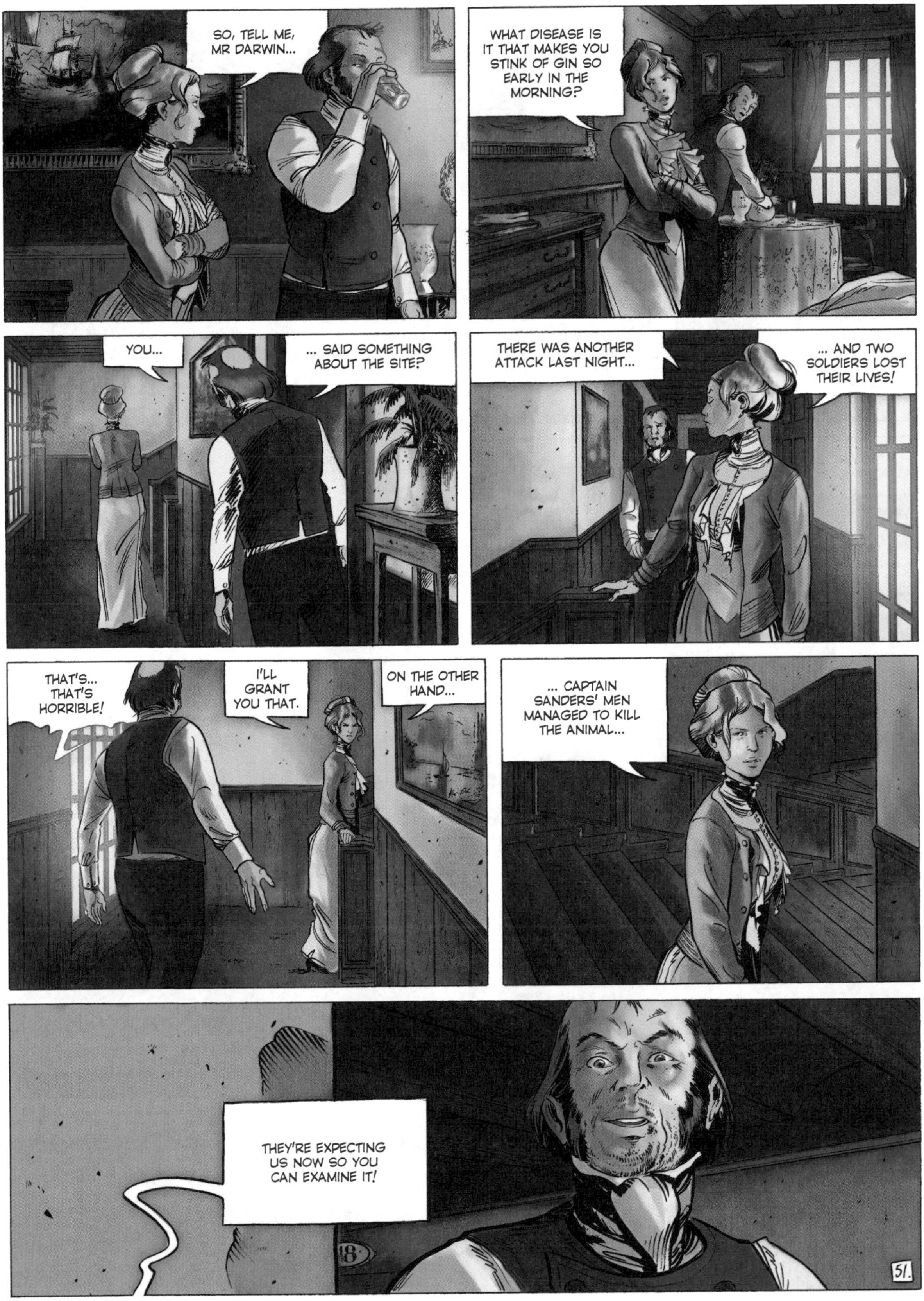

SO, TELL ME, MR DARWIN...
WHAT DISEASE IS IT THAT MAKES YOU STINK OF GIN SO EARLY IN THE MORNING?
YOU...
... SAID SOMETHING ABOUT THE SITE?
THERE WAS ANOTHER ATTACK LAST NIGHT...
... AND TWO SOLDIERS LOST THEIR LIVES!
THAT'S... THAT'S HORRIBLE!
I'LL GRANT YOU THAT.
ON THE OTHER HAND...
... CAPTAIN SANDERS' MEN MANAGED TO KILL THE ANIMAL...
THEY'RE EXPECTING US NOW SO YOU CAN EXAMINE IT!
51.

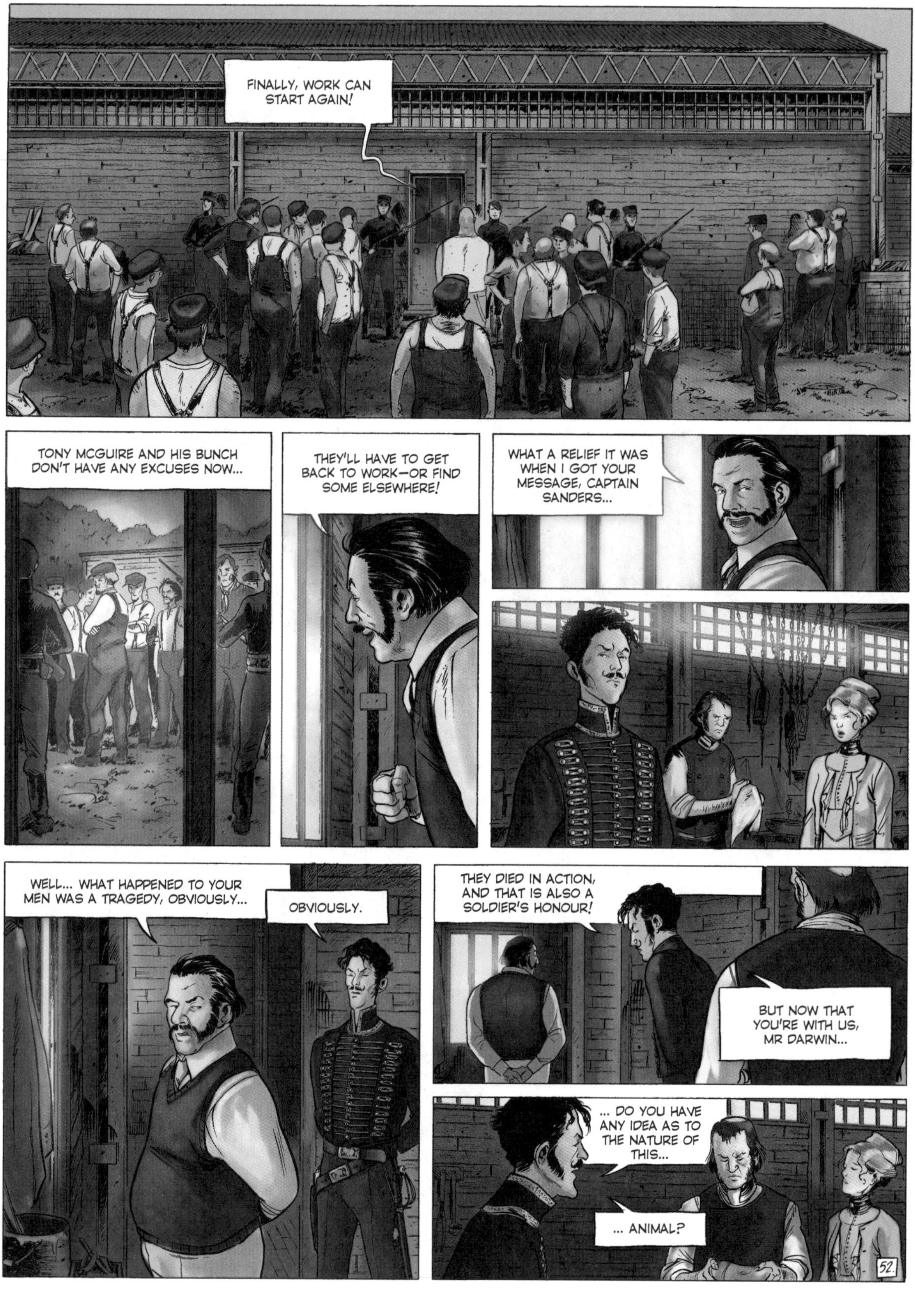
FINALLY, WORK CAN START AGAIN!
TONY MCGUIRE AND HIS BUNCH DON'T HAVE ANY EXCUSES NOW...
THEY'LL HAVE TO GET BACK TO WORK—OR FIND SOME ELSEWHERE!
WHAT A RELIEF IT WAS WHEN I GOT YOUR MESSAGE, CAPTAIN SANDERS...
WELL... WHAT HAPPENED TO YOUR MEN WAS A TRAGEDY, OBVIOUSLY...
OBVIOUSLY.
THEY DIED IN ACTION, AND THAT IS ALSO A SOLDIER'S HONOUR!
BUT NOW THAT YOU'RE WITH US, MR DARWIN...
... DO YOU HAVE ANY IDEA AS TO THE NATURE OF THIS...
... ANIMAL?
52.

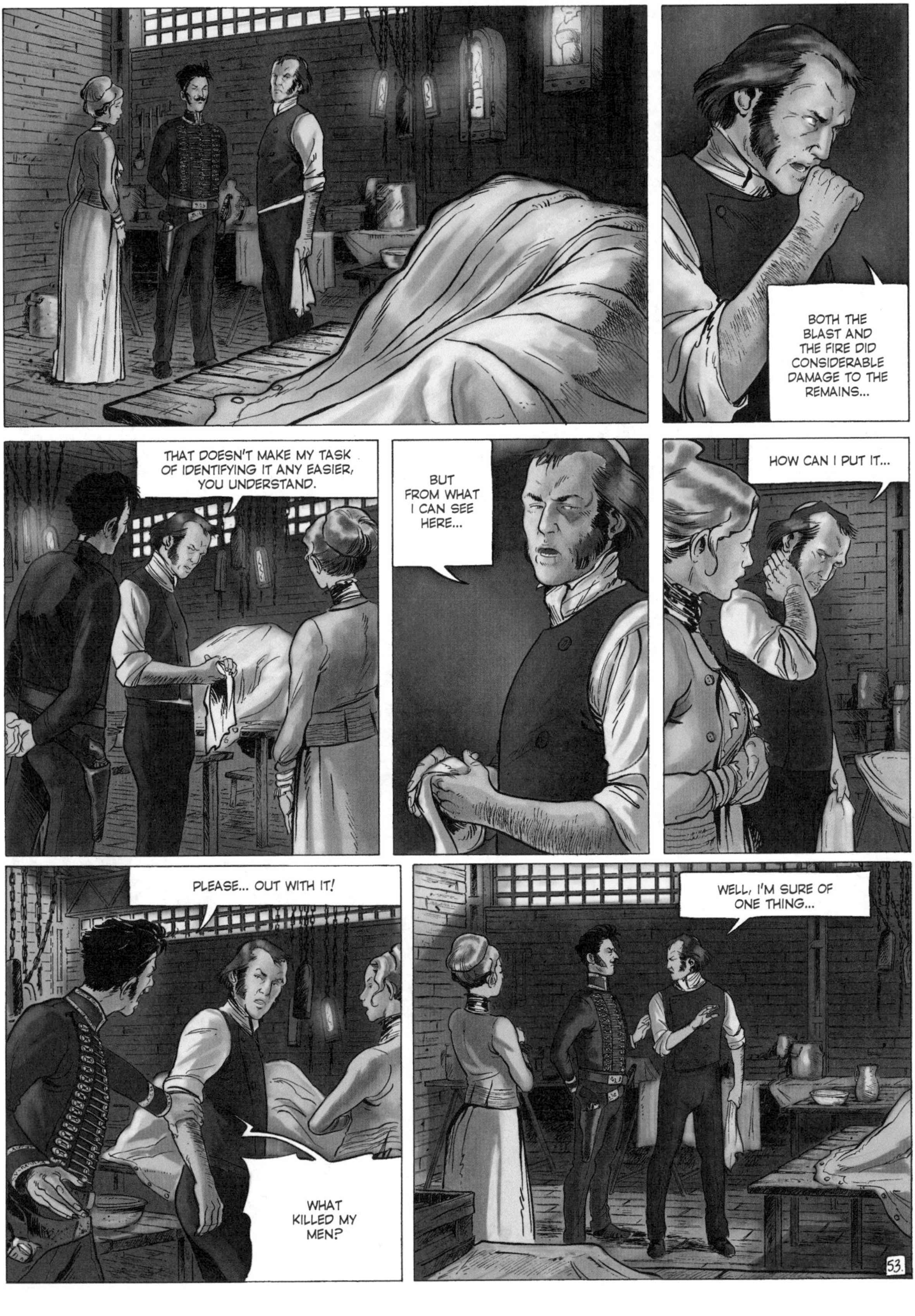
BOTH THE BLAST AND THE FIRE DID CONSIDERABLE DAMAGE TO THE REMAINS...
THAT DOESN'T MAKE MY TASK OF IDENTIFYING IT ANY EASIER, YOU UNDERSTAND.
BUT FROM WHAT I CAN SEE HERE...
HOW CAN I PUT IT...
PLEASE... OUT WITH IT!
WHAT KILLED MY MEN?
WELL, I'M SURE OF ONE THING...
53.

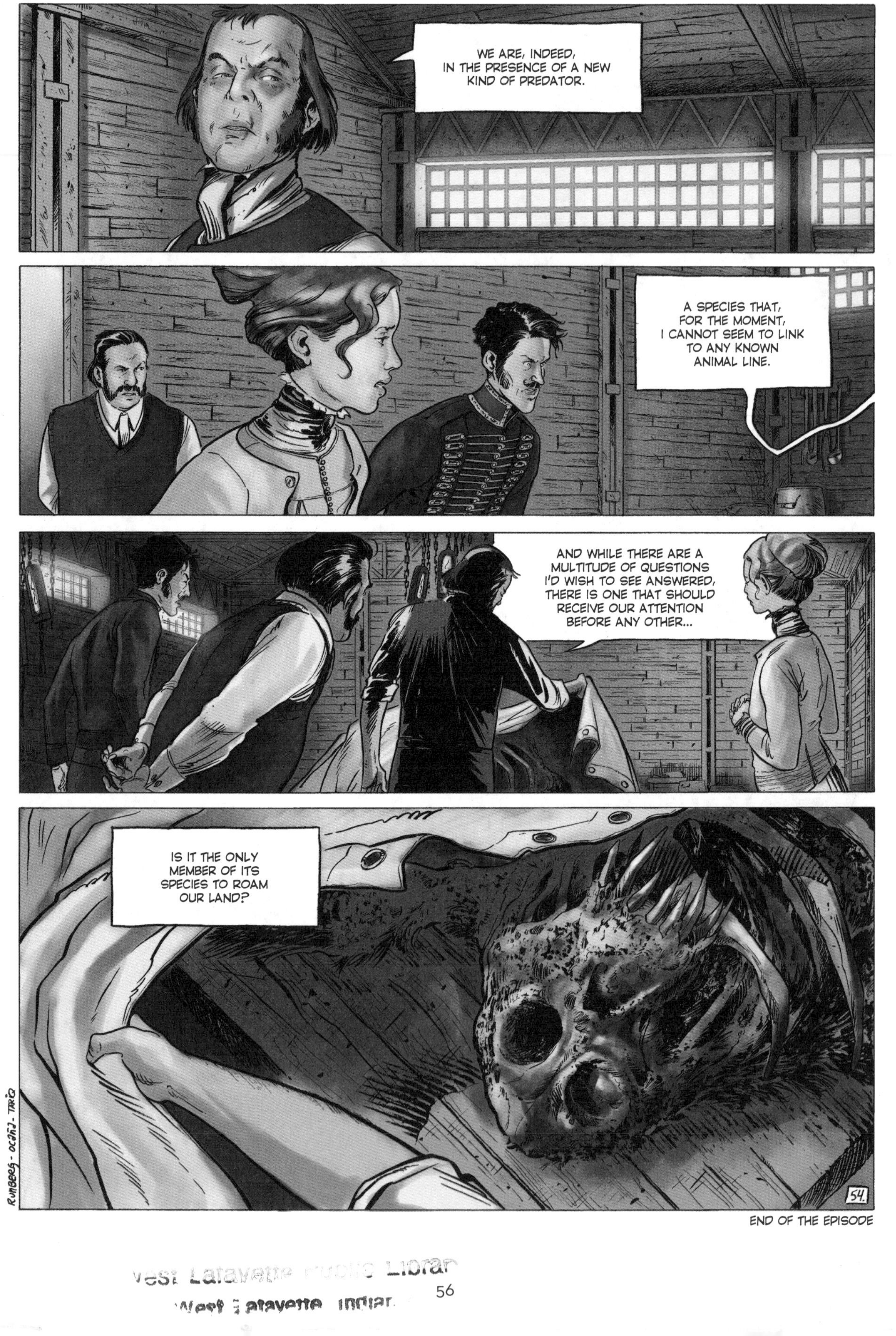
WE ARE, INDEED, IN THE PRESENCE OF A NEW KIND OF PREDATOR.
A SPECIES THAT, FOR THE MOMENT, I CANNOT SEEM TO LINK TO ANY KNOWN ANIMAL LINE.
AND WHILE THERE ARE A MULTITUDE OF QUESTIONS I'D WISH TO SEE ANSWERED, THERE IS ONE THAT SHOULD RECEIVE OUR ATTENTION BEFORE ANY OTHER...
IS IT THE ONLY MEMBER OF ITS SPECIES TO ROAM OUR LAND?
54.

END OF THE EPISODE